The Spin

ISBN 1-86958-442-2

© 1996

Published in 1996 by Hodder Moa Beckett Publishers Limited
[a member of the Hodder Headline Group]
4 Whetu Place, Mairangi Bay, Auckland, New Zealand

Printed by Wright & Carman (NZ) Ltd, Upper Hutt

The Spin

Anonymous

Hodder Moa Beckett

A Novel of New Zealand Politics

Foreword

This is an exercise in political science fiction, an exploration of a parallel electoral universe or, perhaps, our own sometime in the future. It is a place where the dark side of politics dominates.

The leaders of this realm are thankfully not our own and that simple fact should make us all grateful for the real politicians who do inhabit our world. Some of them may be morally or politically bankrupt, but none are this corrupt. They are not that interesting.

The political parties depicted are simply the classic models of socialist left, social democrat, populist centre and right-wing conservatives and, while some will no doubt attempt to draw parallels, no reference is intended to any specific parties in existence.

All characters and events are fictitious. Anyone who finds any resemblance between themselves and anyone in this story is one sick puppy.

1
The Spin

The dimpled bottle of malt scotch whisky on the kitchen table was one-third empty, although, no doubt, the Prime Minister would regard it as two-thirds full. The distinguished leader of the nation, Don Murdoch, was an eternal optimist who had built an entire political career out of looking on the bright side.

The man with him, looking with a little longing at the scotch, was by nature more of a pessimist. It was a disposition he usually sought to suppress, for the increasingly thirsty Ben Bradshaw's job was to create the bright side for Murdoch to exploit. He was the Prime Minister's media strategist, known colloquially as a spin doctor.

Short, balding, with an expanding waistline and a cheerful round face, he could generally accomplish an act of artificial joviality with ease, but tonight it was more difficult. He had never before presided over the death throes of a government. While he might be expert at turning disasters into triumphs, successfully salvaging this particular fiasco would require a direct act of divine intervention and it had been a very long time since Benjamin Bradshaw had last been to Mass.

He stared at the television screen in the distance. The results that flashed across the flickering tube proved the old warhorse Donald Murdoch and his party had tonight suffered a clear loss. You did not have to have a black belt in the political arts to work out his Conservative Party was five seats short of being able to form a majority government.

Yet a smiling Prime Minister was talking of a victory. "By far the largest party in the House, Ben," he said as he drained his glass. "Twice the size of any other single party."

"But still a minority, boss."

Outside, in the cavernous country hall, the large-screen television on the raised wooden stage showed a grossly inflated Ian Fraser gravely shaking his neatly tonsured head. "The nation has spoken but not as clearly as Prime Minister Murdoch would like." Fraser uttered the last few words with a cheerful smirk that rankled.

Ben's irritation was more than likely a small, bitter, tweak of envy. There was more than a slight edge of self-justification in his sudden thought that at least he, Ben Bradshaw, had the sense to know when his day had been and gone. He had extracted himself from the quagmire of Avalon before it had swallowed him whole and he had stumbled with relief into the marginally more honest business of public relations.

He could not help but notice the beaming Fraser still showed every sign of enjoying the swamp. The presenter was positively chortling with excitement as he turned to the political scientist across the studio, demanding, "Nigel, what does this mean for the Government?"

"Who bloody cares what you think, Nigel," Ben muttered morosely, quickly stomping across the kitchen to slam the sliding door shut, cutting off the sight and sound of the broadcast. Right now the only opinion that counted was the one from the old man opposite him leaning on the worn fake grey marble formica table. Murdoch's jacket hung over the back of his chair; the top button on his shirt was open and his tie loose, and his trademark tortoiseshell glasses were perched on the end of his nose.

He was almost seventy and the hard seven-day weeks of intensive campaigning, fourteen hours a day, had taken their toll. He was slightly punchdrunk. There again, he may simply have been a little drunk. Whatever the case, the

Prime Minister relished every strenuous effort that had brought him to this point.

Don Murdoch came from original pioneer stock that made a virtue out of rising at daybreak to burn scrub and carve farming dynasties out of rolling hills and dense bush. Ben suspected it was Murdoch ancestors who had built the famous but pointless Bridge to Nowhere. It was a futile span of redundant concrete across a blind ravine, utterly cut off from civilisation and pointed in the direction of nothing but wilderness. Yet it was a marvel of sheer engineering obstinacy.

"Still, I suppose it's always there if we need it," Murdoch had once somewhat defensively confided to him while on a tour of the upper reaches of the Whanganui River. Ben considered his suspicions about the construction were justified by that remark alone.

Murdoch approached the election campaign with the slash and burn mentality familiar to his Victorian forebears, dropping into bed late at night exhausted by his labours with a belly full of malt whisky to dull the pain. It was how he had always approached the business of getting elected and staying in power. He was a slow-moving bulldozer of a man who ground down those who opposed him, relying on his weight and momentum to carry him forward. Thought was only a secondary process at the best of times for Don Murdoch and, after weeks on the road, the Prime Minister had given up trying to think his way out of the situation he now found himself in.

Ben knew in a few minutes that Murdoch would suck in his gut, smooth his bright white classic short back 'n' sides hair, flick the dandruff off the rounded shoulders of his favourite blue woollen suit and stride onto the stage of the crowded home-town hall. He would beam triumphantly across the heads of the flock of journalists stretching their microphones towards him in supplication. He would wave lustily at the cheering local party faithful, most of whom he had been to primary school with, and his weathered face would slowly traverse half a dozen television cameras like a rusty tank turret.

At that moment Donald Henry Murdoch would make direct, honest eye contact with three million people at home in their living rooms and lie through his teeth. Expertly.

"Three more years! The people have given us the moral mandate to govern for three more years. I expect the support and mature assistance of the opposition minority parties in enabling this." He was rehearsing it already. "How's the grammar, Ben?"

"The grammar is adequate, it's the logic that's faulty. You can't bluff your way through this one."

Murdoch laughed, a coarse throaty cackle, and reached for the bottle.

"That is number four, Don," came the quiet gentle reminder from Faith.

The Prime Minister winked at Ben. "Now, Faith, you know I could have fourteen and it wouldn't make a scrap of difference."

Actually, it did. His "wouldn't" sounded like "wooden". His tongue seemed to swell to twice its normal size after even one whisky. Fortunately, the Prime Minister always had at least one shot early in the day and most people thought his speech was naturally slurred.

He liked being called "Prime Minister". Shortly after Ben took the job, Murdoch told him he could also call him "sir", if he wanted. Ben stuck to calling him Prime Minister.

He had been known to refer to him as "boss" in wild moments of intimacy and "the fool" in instants of frequent frustration.

They had known each other, in a guarded sort of way, for twenty years. In another age, in another life, Ben had worked as a journalist in Parliament's press gallery. As a reporter he had chattily called the young backbencher Don to his face and, come to think of it, a lot worse. That changed once Murdoch became first a party leader and then prime minister. Once Ben entered his employ the gulf between them widened even further. The adherence to honorifics was not pomposity, although Murdoch was surely afflicted with a mammoth share of that, too. It was just that he was just a man who believed in the master-servant relationship. As long as he was master.

When he was a parliamentary reporter Bradshaw may have been something approximating an equal to Murdoch the backbencher. They still maintained an easy rapport later in Murdoch's less than meteoric career when Ben followed the new prime minister abroad on one of the endless political junkets the man in his bottomless vanity liked to call summits.

That was a ridiculously over-inflated view of the meetings. He played molehill to other leaders' mountains and the US president would not have been able to recall Murdoch's name five minutes after squeezing his hand at the inevitable photo opportunity that followed every so-called bilateral discussion. Actually, if Ben thought about it, on the two occasions they saw that particular president at the White House the most powerful man in the world had trouble remembering his own name.

Murdoch's position in the international pecking order

may not have been high, but as a political aide Ben occupied an even lower slot in the foodchain. Once he joined the staff he walked three paces behind, carried the bags and knew his place as a hired hand.

Don Murdoch had a prefect mentality, of the kind borne later in life by those who never achieved such an exalted state at high school. Certainly achievement and success came slowly to him. Whenever he gained some small morsel of status, he hoarded it and let everyone feel the distance it put between them.

Only Faith was exempt from this conceit. A tall, thin, raw-boned woman with greying hair, she looked like the long suffering share-milker's wife she had once been and, perhaps, should have remained. Anything Don had now become he owed to Faith's sacrifice. He knew it and, accordingly, there was seldom any real distance between them. It was inevitable that she should be here now, in the inner sanctum of the battered yellowed kitchen at the back of the community hall on election night watching quietly as the big white water-heater on the wall came to the boil, preparing another vat of tea for the troops. Thirty years of reasonably happy marriage appeared to have bonded the Murdochs like superglue.

The caterers for the long night's victory celebrations had been evicted as soon as the first ten percent of party votes were counted. The Prime Minister's entourage could have stayed back in the old Murdoch family homestead on the edge of the state highway just out of town until they were sure of the result but, such was the man's confidence in his own infallibility, he had insisted they head for the hall early. From the moment the news turned ugly the kitchen became the command bunker for the PM and his staff.

Actually, most of the staffers had also been spat out of the kitchen, one by one, on search and destroy missions. The two press secretaries had been sent off to apply some spin to the hacks because the journalists were morbidly picking over the carcass of the rapidly disintegrating victory celebrations. Left alone for too long, reporters became bored and dangerously inquisitive. There was a volatile mixture brewing in the hall because the party loyalists had stopped dancing and were morosely attacking the well-stocked bar to wash away the sour taste of the night's reversal. Left alone for too long to mingle with the sneering media, the liquored up supporters would explode.

Ronald, the personal private secretary, and his assistant were dispatched to the communications centre in the caretaker's small office. Beside the mops, the brooms and the detergent were several specially installed phone lines and the secretaries' precautionary mission was to remain ready to contact the Governor-General, the Governor of the Reserve Bank, three key cabinet ministers, the party president and the Conservative Party's chief number cruncher at Dominion Headquarters should their advice be required. Not that Don Murdoch was, of course, the kind of man who sought advice readily. He preferred to hear his own prejudices recycled back to him and would only absorb a suggestion from someone when it was sugar-coated as a casual aside that Murdoch could appropriate and later claim as his own.

There was a sharp squeal from the rusty sliding door as Simon Small swept back into the room. A dapper little man with ice cold eyes, his grandiose title was Chief of Staff for the Prime Minister's Office. It was a job description he had created for himself. Ben maintained that the words Chief

Kneecapper, Plotter and Schemer would have been more accurate depiction of Small's role.

"Shouldn't you be with the other press secs, Bradshaw?" he fired as an aside. "Feeding the chooks?"

Ben beamed a telepathic stream of venom at him. I am not a press secretary, he thought, I am not even the chief press secretary because passing out press releases is someone else's job, is it not, Simon. I am the Prime Minister's media strategist and senior planning advisor. You unmitigated arsehole. That signal sent, he told Small in his politest voice, "Peter and Julie are quite capable of dealing with the press gallery, Simon." The tall, grey-haired Peter Jackson headed the press office and commanded warm respect from the otherwise viciously suspicious hacks. Julie, who acted as an assistant to both Ben and Peter, was also skilled at smoothing the ruffled feathers of political reporters. The men regarded her with unrequited lust, the women knew her as a friend who could be trusted. While Peter and Julie were a good team, Ben was not about to be lumped in with mere peddlers of the Government's message. He took pride in being the message maker and shaper.

Murdoch felt the chill between his advisors cut through the warmth of the scotch and he rumbled at Simon Small, "I want Ben here."

"Scum," Small said somewhat ambiguously. Ben gave him the benefit of the doubt and presumed the scum referred to was Her Majesty's Loyal Press Gallery, otherwise known as the chooks. Briefings and press conferences were occasions often referred to as "feeding the chooks".

"The fickle bastards have already written us off. As I came back they were all saying they should be at bloody Christopher Cross's Freedom Party headquarters or with

Foot's Liberals. Anywhere but here," he huffed. "You know, it was the bloody Maoris that did us in. The Treaty issue. You saw how our party vote took a dive in the rural electorates and down in the South Island. I told you all along, they think we're too soft on Treaty claims.We should have canned the damn Waitangi Tribunal and taken a hard line."

"And mortgaged our children's future for short term political gain, Simon?" Ben said drily.

"And been realistic!" Simon snapped back.

Murdoch shook his head. "We were right, Simon. We did the right thing and if it costs us the government then so be it."

Small flicked him a scathing look and changed the subject, slipping into his most authoritative voice. "Now, Prime Minister, I've been talking to Jane Street . . ."

"I hope you used one of the land lines, Simon. You used a standard telephone?" The alarm bells were sounding for the eternally vigilant Bradshaw. He endlessly lectured all the PM's staff on the dangers of cellphone conversations being intercepted.

"My phone is perfectly secure," Small sniffed, patting his pinstriped pocket.

"It is not secure, Simon. Whether it is analogue or even digital, eavesdroppers can listen to your mobile phone calls." Ben was getting heated. Better than most people Ben knew that, in addition to strange men from the ministry, media, opposition parties, foreign embassies, money market dealers, freaky geeks who drive around in four-wheel-drive vehicles and heavily armed disgruntled former postal employees – all of whom had radio scanners and habitually listened to cellphone traffic – there were people tuned in to such calls who might cause serious trouble.

"The better equipped of them can easily decrypt even the more technologically advanced digital calls and on that thing you're carrying right now, you can bet everything you said just then to the Minister of Finance is going out on a news wire service somewhere."

Simon blinked briefly and ignored the telecommunications tutorial. "She wants you to call her urgently, Prime Minister."

"Bugger the battleaxe," Murdoch snapped. "Two seconds after you hung up she'll be on that didgeridoologue phone you're talking about, doing a head count in caucus, wondering if she can engineer a spill and insert her own fat bum in my place. She can wait."

This was a neat and unerringly accurate analysis of his right-hand person, the formidable Finance Minister Jane Street. She was a big woman with even bigger hair, and her flaming red mane signalled a propensity for quite ferocious outbursts of temper. The sainted Faith would have described her, sympathetically, as a big-boned girl. The matronly Street led the small but powerful monetarist faction in Cabinet. Although the Prime Minister saw her fearsome grip on the Treasury pursestrings in another light: "Monetarist, my arse. She's just tight as a fish's bum by nature."

The media pack liked to portray her as utterly dominating Murdoch on policy matters but those in the inner circle of the Beehive knew Street was awesomely, icily disapproving of Murdoch's occasional rebellious bouts of pragmatism, which she saw as a tendency to dangerous expediency. He, in turn, loathed her in an utterly uncomplicated way.

"She'd have made a great prop," he laughed. "Imagine Bull Allen trying to take a tight head off her, Ben."

Pleased to be included in the discussion, Ben noted with some small satisfaction that Simon Small was now extremely irritated.

"She has a great brain, Prime Minister," said Small.

"Simon, that's like saying she has a nice personality," Murdoch roared.

"Nice brain, shame about the two faces." Ben enjoyed tweaking Small even further.

Faith's disapproving shuffle at the teapot brought an end to the Street-bashing and the talk turned to what to do next.

"Prime Minister, Mrs Street says, and I agree, it is imperative we establish a working coalition tonight. Before you confront the press and the television cameras."

"Why on earth should I do that, Simon?" Murdoch still retained a grin. "I've got nearly eight weeks to work out how to gain a full majority in the House. You might be surprised what we can pull off in that time."

"We've been through this before, PM. As Jane, ah, Mrs Street has repeatedly stressed. The financial markets in New York are still open tonight and they are trading. Even tomorrow there will be no respite. Their screens may not be working but the dealers will. They'll be trading informally right through Sunday. All day."

Murdoch took a swallow from the large tumbler and watched Simon pacing the kitchen floor, slicing the air with his hand as he tried to impress on them how urgent he believed the situation had become.

"You have no idea of the economic pressure that is building, a pressure that will only be relieved by the formation of a stable government committed to the kind of policies our Government has been responsible for." Small took a breath.

"Damn fine drop of scotch, just what the doctor ordered." Murdoch could be infuriating when he chose and at that moment he chose to annoy Simon Small.

"I'll get Christopher Cross on the phone for you," the increasingly testy Chief of Staff suggested, "although he will demand the earth. Tell him to forget it. Without you he's history. Give him no more than four seats in Cabinet. Don't give him Finance, of course. The markets really would wet themselves if you did that."

Simon Small raced on, ignoring the appalled look he was getting from his leader. Murdoch's glass had frozen in its travels half way to his mouth. "Education, Health, Welfare and Housing would be perfect portfolios to give away. Four jobs guaranteed to fast-track him and his bloody Freedom Party into oblivion. The public will wind up hating his guts." Small waved an arm in benign dismissal of the great unwashed. He went on. "We control the Budget. He won't be able to deliver on those absurd promises he's made and, voila, he's finished. In six months he and the rest of them will be rating the big doughnut in the polls. Zero. Zip. Nada."

Simon Small was supposed to be smart. A top lawyer in a sizable Wellington practice until his partners could stand him no longer and they slipped him the knife, he was on record as saying he could not start a day till he had had a fight with someone. One morning, after a decade in the firm he helped create, he woke up a lot richer from the payoff but without a job and with no one left to argue with.

Realising his golden parachute from the partners would

not last longer than his wife's next shopping trip to Sydney, Simon cast around for a new career in which his vindictive talents would be better appreciated. Then it came to him. As a lawyer he had saved the Government's hide in more than one High Court case, and he had ensured several, more personal, ministerial mishaps were kept out of the hands of an ungrateful judiciary and Police Department. So Small cashed in his political insurance policy for a job in the Prime Minister's Office.

He took to it like a shark to the Freyberg Pool. Pinned to the corkboard beside his desk was Chuck Colson's famous motto, 'When you have them by the balls, their hearts and minds will follow.' The former Nixon aide probably said it jokingly. Small was serious.

Yet, however tough and devious Simon Small might consider himself to be, his boss proved to be a harder man. Don Murdoch was publicly perceived as a dull plodder of limited intellectual resources, but privately even his closest associates would agree no one can rise to the top of the Beehive without a postgraduate degree in ruthless street cunning.

Murdoch was acutely aware that many of those around him possessed far quicker wits than he. His best defence, like so many other poor managers, was to divide and rule. Murdoch was content to play Simon off against Ben, knowing that they would be too busy hating each other to hatch plots to mislead or control him. It was not a highly efficient system but everyone in the inner circle did fulfil a necessary role. Faith was his backbone, Ben his conscience, Simon his gonads.

Ironically, Ben realised, any second now Simon was going to have his own nuts cracked, because Don Murdoch detested being told what to do. Especially when he was being told to kiss and make up with a man he considered his most bitter rival.

"Cross is not an option," Murdoch barked.

"Prime Minister . . ."

"Don't preach to me!" His face flushed a deep red, he thumped the flat of his hefty hand on the table. Faith jumped, Ben flinched, Small's eyes simply narrowed as they were caught in the lava flow of the man's volcanic hatred of Chris Cross.

"He was in my caucus for years and all the bugger did was hunt headlines. Don't tell me about Christopher bloody Cross." He almost choked on the name. "He was lazy. He was treacherous. He did nothing unless it was for his own benefit. A liar. A cheat." He looked sideways at Faith for approval. "A womaniser," he spat in disgust.

Faith looked over her shoulder as she struggled to cut off the steadily rising shriek of the water-heater's whistle and shook her head either in shared revulsion or bewilderment at her husband's blind prejudice against Cross. It was certainly hard to tell which was emitting more steam, Murdoch or the ancient Zip.

"He . . . he . . ." Don was grasping for words to sum up the bottomless depths of his hatred for the opposition party leader. "When he couldn't have my party he sold it down the river and started his own."

The slightly disloyal thought came to Ben that Chris had also committed the cardinal sin of consistently outrating dear old Don in the preferred Prime Minister stakes for most of the last few years. Such apparently effortless success was not a career-enhancing option when a man like Murdoch was leader.

"You don't have to love him," Simon persisted. "You don't

have to like him. You don't even have to trust him. Just take him into your Cabinet."

Ben decided Small might be a sleazeball but that did not mean he lacked courage.

Despite the PM's almost homicidal wrath, the Chief of Staff went on stubbornly. "Make him your coalition partner. We'll slowly screw him. Destroy him. By the time he cracks we'll be strong enough for a snap election that we can win in our own right."

Through the closed door came a loud groan of despair from the crowd. The final results were through, confirming what those in the kitchen had known for the last hour. The Government remained at least five seats short of a clear majority.

Murdoch ran his fingers through his silvered hair and snorted. "Even if I took him on, the markets would go crazy. The money men hate him with a vengeance. Christopher Cross is economic death to big business."

Wrong again, Don, you don't know how wrong you are. Ben's mind raced back to a conversation several months before in a tiny coffee bar across the road from the Beehive.

2
The Spin

"**H**e's fantastic in the sack," Susan said, lighting a Dunhill.

"Oh, for God's sake." Ben's ruddy face flushed even darker as he shuffled his chair away from the cafe table in exasperation and stared out the window at the traffic accelerating away from the intersection up Bowen Street.

"Oh, baby, nobody does it like Chris," she crooned mockingly.

"You are disgusting."

"And you are being adolescent," she insisted briskly, switching in an instant from the seductive deep sultry voice she had used a moment before. "If you are going to get jealous, why ask me what I see in him? Why ask stupid questions like, do I love him? You don't have to marry someone to sleep with them, Ben."

In that regard she was definitely talking to the wrong person. *Metro* magazine's gossipy rodent had once described Ben Bradshaw as 'a serial monogamist'. Four wives and a series of impossibly young girlfriends seemed obscenely excessive to the Ferret but each had truly seemed the Great Love of Ben's life. Every relationship made extraordinary sense at the time, however short that time may have been.

Ben would never be described as a good-looking man, but he had wit and charm on his side. More than that, he genuinely liked women, he thrived in their company. They sensed this and reciprocated. Many heterosexual men of his age innately distrusted women and sought only conquests, women they could control or dominate. Ben was content to enjoy and appreciate women in the same way he appreciated so many fine works of God and Man. A beautiful woman with a brain to match held an unbeatable attraction. Although, if pressed, he might admit good food, fine wine, quality art and his old black Porsche 911S were close contenders.

"Don't mention my marriages," he moaned. "They're like tornadoes: they start with a hiss and a roar and then you end up losing half your house."

"I've heard that one before. Lord, Ben, how often does someone like Chris come along? He's bright, he's good-looking, interesting and, I won't deny it, power is an aphrodisiac. Look, if it makes you feel any better he is so stressed out and works so late we hardly ever actually" – she paused, looking for a less painful expression – "get boats in harbours, if you know what I mean."

Ugh. He groaned inwardly. "Your docking manoeuvres wouldn't be helped by the fact he drinks almost as much as my man, Murdoch." He vigorously stirred the latte. "Chris has a drinking problem. You know that?"

"And you have an obsessional love problem. You know that? You only want me because you know you can't have me." Susan checked the small gold Cartier watch Cross had brought back for her from some taxpayer funded trip to the United States. She gathered her handbag from the floor, adding, "Besides, it would never work. You and me, I mean."

Ben had heard that often before and, as it turned out, the women who said it were inevitably right. It never worked in the long run. Yet, in saying it, those women were sometimes signalling a tiny, hidden curiosity that 'it' might work.

A small breeze of hope fanned his dampened interest and he cunningly switched from dissecting her love affair to a subject he thought might hold her attention a little longer.

"Yes, I'd better get a move on, too." He feigned looking around for the bill. "I have a campaign committee meeting."

"Campaign committee? The election is still nearly six months away. You're having campaign strategy meetings now? How often? Is this the first?" The bag dropped back on the lino. "Who is chairing it? Murdoch?"

"Who else would you expect?" Ben had her full attention now. He warned her, "I don't want to hear this on the breakfast news tomorrow, Susan."

Her eyes widened in a well-practised look of innocence. Susan Lewis was one of the most dangerous journalists cruising the shallow waters of the press gallery. A mass of dark curly hair framed a guileless heart-shaped face and she had the kind of body that seemed to have gone out of fashion with Marilyn Monroe. Susan was in her early thirties, pale skinned with a fabulously pneumatic bust, narrow waist and rounded hips. In an era of the modishly anorexic the voluptuous Susan had the kind of beauty that appealed enormously to men of a certain age. They expected her to be a poopsie and she played to that prejudice, in the process extracting the most remarkable utterances from otherwise unremarkable men. Crusty cabinet ministers who would eat Paul Holmes for breakfast found themselves choking on their Ricies when they heard their lapses replayed over the radio in her morning newscasts from Parliament.

"We've been meeting for the last month," confessed Ben, warming to the gossip. "Murdoch, Simon Small, me, the Deputy PM, Jane Street, a couple of guys from the ad agency, plus Ernie Watts."

Susan raised an eyebrow.

"We have to have him. Murdoch may hate him but Ernie is the party president." He added casually, "Oh, and from time to time, Clarry Evans."

"Evans!" Susan shrilled. This surprised her, as Ben knew it would. Evans was her boss, the chairman of the board of her own radio network.

"Well, he does the fundraising." Ben grinned. "Someone has to run the chook raffles and Clarry does it better than anyone else."

"Chook raffles! Ha! Stuffing fat six-figure cheques into a briefcase is not running frozen chicken raffles. I always knew he was the party bagman. Evans knows the corporates better than anyone else and why else would you guys give him all those cosy jobs on Government boards unless there was something in it for you. Raffles," she laughed. "How much has he salted away so far?"

"We give plenty of people who never do anything for us cosy jobs on quangos." He tried to evade her probing by mounting a sterling defence of Clarry's undoubtedly able management ability. Evans had few formal business qualifications yet had proved himself an extremely capable executive. His rise through various quangos and other Government-controlled boards had been impressive over the last two decades.

Of course, the personal connections Clarry Evans cultivated with several highly ranked individuals in the Conservative Party had not hindered his career. A cheery, affable chap, Clarry was highly adept at networking and it was only natural the party should turn to him when there was a particularly difficult task to perform. Out of loyalty to his friends and to the party and for the six-figure sum involved in chairing the running of a sensitive State Owned Enterprise, Clarry was always willing to lend a helping hand.

Still, nothing succeeds like success and nothing is so

lonesome as failure. Had Clarry failed to perform or proved abysmally incompetent, the party would have discarded him like a used Kleenex. Clarry had earned his 'most favoured' status on the boards and committees of the Government's gravy train. In fact, he was still working his way through the entree: he had control of the socially prestigious state radio network, a peg up the social ladder his wife enjoyed, but Clarry had his eye on a much more nutritious main course – control of Television, Energy, Treasury or even the Reserve Bank.

Susan maintained a healthy contempt for the people who ran her radio network. Like most journalists she was determinedly middle class in her aspirations, liberal in her social attitudes but decidedly left wing, almost anarchistic, in her attitude to authority. She was also not easily led astray from a line of inquiry.

"How much have the party got, Benny? How much has Clarry squirrelled away for you guys?"

"Enough to run the campaign."

"You have that in hand already? You're talking three . . . no . . . maybe four million dollars. You have that kind of money at your disposal?" Susan was impressed.

"Your boy Chris did it all for us. They are so terrified of Christopher Cross that Clarry has to beat the big money boys off with a stick."

Susan smiled, her dark Cupid lips pursing as she bit off something she almost said.

"Yes?" Ben waited. Trading confidences took patience.

"Maybe they are not as terrified of Chris as you may think," she murmured, looking into her empty cup.

"Maybe they're having a bob each way, you mean?" He tried to not let his interest show.

"Mmmm." She was nervously looking at her watch again.

"We should talk some more, Susan." Any more oil in his voice and his cholesterol levels would have gone into the red danger zone.

"I don't think so," she said briskly. Susan regretted her slip in telling tales out of school or, in this case, out of bed.

With a twinge of jealousy it occurred to Ben that if boats were not entering harbours then there was obviously plenty of time remaining for intimate conversation with Chris. In the world of politics an exchange of gossip could be a worse betrayal than an act of adultery.

She found her handbag and slid off the chair in a fluid movement. "I mustn't keep you from your meeting."

"And I must not keep you from your assignation," he sniped sarcastically. The Freedom Party caucus would be breaking for lunch and Cross was probably heading across Molesworth Street to his flat for a cup of tea and a lie down. A crowded hour with Susan, then back to the House.

The barest trace of pink tinged her cheeks as she did her best to ignore the wisecrack. The eyelashes did a frantic flutter of bewilderment and she swept out of the cafe. Pausing briefly at the kerb, thick curls swirling in the stiff southerly, she wrestled with the decision whether or not to cross under his gaze. Her brazen instincts won and she marched past the war memorial towards the bottom of Molesworth Street and Cross's flat.

As he wandered back through Bowen House, Ben ruefully wondered how Chris's post-caucus stress levels were holding out. Poorly, he hoped. I am a masochist, he decided; to dwell on the carnal nature of Susan's affair was pointless. Was it that she was so unobtainable? Was it simply that she was the woman of his old friend and rival, Christopher Cross? What was it about Susan that held such an attraction?

Her intellect was sharp. She tempered a healthy cynicism about politics with a measure of idealism. In her work she took none too subtle editorial stances on wrongs perpetrated by the Government against the homeless, the sick and the elderly. For a woman who could conduct a clandestine affair with a married man she had a surprisingly moral streak.

For a man, Ben was reasonably intuitive. He knew, for example, why he loathed Simon Small. The Bradshaws had been a Catholic working class family in Wellington's Newtown, respected within the narrow confines of their own community. His father had been a plumber but, to the elder Bradshaw's eternal disgust, Ben had rejected an apprenticeship, preferring to stay on at St Pat's to do a scholarship that took him, finally, to university in Auckland. He had further earned his father's contempt by doing a "useless" history degree and compounded the sin by leaving before he completed the course, becoming a cadet reporter on the old *Auckland Star*. Mr Bradshaw never read anything other than the weekly edition of *Truth* and consequently had a poor opinion of journalism.

Simon Small came from a different New Zealand, north of the Bombay Hills. He attended King's College and when he left university his father, who was a judge, ensured he found a job in a prominent Queen Street law firm. The only time he mildly disappointed the learned judge was when Simon left to form his own practice, but the disapproval was short-lived for the venture quickly prospered thanks to the combined Small family connections.

When the two men met Simon's first question to Ben had been, "Where did you go to school?" Ben told him honestly and felt the shutters drop in response.

Perhaps it was a sense of a shared background that was the source of Ben's manic attraction to Susan. She came from Grey Lynn, in its time Auckland's equivalent of Newtown. Her father had been a low-grade career public servant in the local post office. She had poleaxed her parents by leaving her convent school and going to the Auckland Technical Institute, graduating top of her year's journalism course. They had lived parallel lives, a decade apart.

If Ben could ever penetrate the barrier of platonic friendship she had erected between them he could foresee a remarkable relationship that might for once endure. In Susan's mind, however, there were only two kinds of men. Those she bedded and those she could be friends with. There could be no cross-over between her categories, he grumbled to himself as he was carried along on the subterranean route of the travelator in a tunnel several metres beneath Bowen Street. It was typical that Parliament should have an escalator that went neither up nor down but took a bland horizontal route hidden from public view.

He waved a cheery hello to George the security guard and stepped into the tiny claustrophobia-inducing confines of a Beehive lift. If he stretched out his arms he could easily brace himself on the brown wool carpet that stretched up the walls to above head height. He did that often, sometimes from claustrophobia, sometimes from drunkenness, usually as a childish indulgence. Sometimes he would trace trivial obscene graffiti in the soft pile of the walls: 'Small sucks' or 'Cross is crap'. He would see if he could complete all the letters of the message before the doors opened under the gaze of the watchful receptionist in the lobby of the ninth floor.

On this occasion as he stepped out, the words 'Cross wanks' were raised in the pile. It was utterly adolescent but he felt better as he called a cheerful "Hi!" to the long-suffering receptionist, who waved a stack of yellow messages at him.

"I'll pick them up on the way back, promise," he fended her off and veered left towards the double swing doors. The campaign committee met in the Prime Minister's office. Such was Murdoch's insecurity he preferred his home turf if there was even a hint of impending argument.

Out of the corner of his eye Ben noticed a shape dart towards him.

Simon Small was pacing the marble floor of the circular central core outside the lifts on the ninth floor. Ben was satisfied to note he looked more than a little liverish, a condition that may have had something to do with a minor Bradshaw victory. Years before, when Small first stormed the bastions of the Beehive, Ben immediately had him banished two floors below the seat of power to the arid wasteland of the seventh floor's even drier advisors.

The head of the Prime Minister's Department, James Brand, had developed a well-founded but almost pathological aversion to Small. It was, for Brand, almost physical. As Superman would crumple when exposed to Kryptonite, so the otherwise steely Brand would wilt and melt when exposed to even a minor dose of Small. Brand, the perfect public servant, could not remain in the same room with a creature as politically crass as Small for more than the few seconds it took for him to make polite excuses between clenched teeth and leave.

There was an eternal division in the Beehive between the public servants who rowed the ship of state and the political appointees who beat the drums and, occasionally, cracked the whip for their masters. The gap between the supposedly neutral officials of the Prime Minister's Department and the nakedly political employees of the Prime Minister's Office was almost unbridgeable.

Individuals from both sides would, however, form shifting coalitions when their interests coincided. There was no office space left on the ninth floor for a late arrival like Small, Ben had told Brand. No room on the eighth either, the bureaucrat fired back. The seventh, perhaps? Snickering, they found a narrow closet between two beancounters from Treasury and consigned Small to the minuscule office. Had it been in Brand's power he would have had contractors seal him inside with concrete.

Now, temporarily freed from his exile and once again allowed within conspiratorial whispering earshot of the Prime Minister, Small was fired with enthusiasm.

"Have you finalised the regional tours?" he snapped. "We have to get them out of the way well before the campaign. By then I want him in Auckland or Wellington every night, within easy reach of the television studios."

"I'm not sure we decided on the levels of TV news exposure that would be helpful during the campaign, Simon."

The media were Ben's territory, not Small's.

"You're not serious? We all agreed last week this is, undoubtedly, the most presidential campaign yet. The Leader's profile is everything when it comes to the party vote."

Small had a curious habit of referring to Murdoch as the Leader. Translated into German, Ben mused, it was Der

Fuhrer. Old Don made an unlikely Hitler but Simon would definitely have been a Brownshirt in the Third Reich. Goebbels, perhaps. No, Himmler.

Ben's amused smile only incensed Simon further. "The party tried to hide him at the last election and look at the near disaster we suffered. He is our only strength!"

"In strength lies victory. Work makes you free. There is a distinctly historic ring to what you say, Simon." Ben smiled archly.

Actually, Small was right, but it was not part of the game to agree too soon. The Chief of Staff stalked through the Private Secretary's office with Ben trailing behind. They marched into Murdoch's suite with Simon still labouring the point.

"The one thing we have learned is that in an MMP election there is no such thing as a marginal seat. Or, if there is, we don't care. Party vote! Party vote! Keep telling yourself, the only thing that counts is the final party vote. The constituency seats are meaningless to a party in the Government's position."

Tell that to our candidates running for seats, thought Ben. Sorry, chaps. You are meaningless in Simon Small's greater scheme of things. Don't expect a dollar from us and the PM can't spare the time to help you win.

They nodded to Murdoch, who rose from behind the huge desk at the end of the room.

"You're right on time." There were too many 'r's in his greeting – Johnny Walker had already paid a morning visit. Ben flinched. They had a Chamber of Commerce luncheon and speech at one o'clock. A couple more scotches downtown with the businessmen and Murdoch would sound positively Highlands in origin.

"We'll stick with the slogan we agreed on," Murdoch declared. "Play Safe. Make Doubly Sure. Tick Conservative Twice. I hear what you're saying, Simon, but you can't forget the boys slugging it out in the trenches. I'm one of them myself."

Murdoch's empathy for the candidates running in the hard-fought constituencies might have sounded genuine but for the fact his own electorate, Tutaekuri on the east coast of the North Island, was one of the Conservative Party's safest seats. Murdoch, of course, also occupied the number-one slot on the party's list. It was a little electoral insurance. Murdoch was more comfortable discussing other people's problems and abhorred talking about, let alone suffering, his own.

"The slogan's too long," said Ben as the three wandered towards the couches and the lanky figure of Deputy Prime Minister Bob Cameron strode past.

The droll Cameron was making his usual hearty noises. "And you are looking fighting fit too, Prime Minister, more than ready for a stiff battle in the electorate. Sorry I can't follow you over the top in the trenches but someone's got to stay behind and look after the women."

"You'd be just the man for the job, Bob," laughed Murdoch.

As deputy leader, Cameron had secured a comfortable position on the list, immediately behind Murdoch. He had thrown in his old constituency seat and, no longer responsible to the bickering old ladies of the electorate branches, was settling back to enjoy the genteel life of a party list MP with no responsibilities beyond enjoying the perks of the job and catering to the many needs of his younger, newer, more demanding second wife. The first Mrs

Cameron died quietly, as uncomplaining in the death throes of breast cancer as she had been throughout her life, sparing the congenitally unfaithful Cameron the nasty repercussions of an ugly divorce. Dutiful to the end.

Murdoch trusted Cameron as much as he trusted anyone. The good-looking deputy leader had perfected laziness as an art form. Seemingly ambitionless and suffering a charisma bypass, Bob Cameron posed no apparent threat to the Prime Minister, an essential ingredient for success in the Murdoch Cabinet.

Cameron's modest denials of his universally acknowledged prowess as a ladykiller were cut short by the loud entrance of a small army of elegantly cut grey suits. The ad men and the party bagmen seemed comfortable together, with the men from the agency chuckling in the wake of the chief fundraisers, party president Ernie Watts and the untiring Government servant Clarry Evans. The group had their own private joke running, which tittered to a halt when Murdoch glared at them, suspicious that the punchline might have involved him.

With the sixth sense of their profession, alert to the Prime Minister's annoyance, the three advertising agency suits switched on several megawatts of charm and launched straight into their "Boy, have we got a campaign for you!" routine.

They flashed large cardboard mock-ups of newspaper ads, waved colourful storyboard sketches of the party's TV commercials and gunned the volume on a small ghetto-blaster. It emitted an appalling country and western wail that was to be the party's election-time theme song. The committee sat expressionless for several minutes as the agency men sweated over their presentation.

"What's all this telling us?" said Murdoch finally. "What's the message?"

"Better the devil you know!" concluded the short fat suit.

"Well," added the taller suit quickly. "It's not quite as blatant as that, but that's the subliminal impact, overall."

"Picture it more as a plea for stability. You know what I mean? It's a straight thrust to the jugular," concluded the boss suit. "We all know what I'm talking about here, don't we? We're feeding people's quest for security."

A few seconds of silence followed the onslaught from the suits. Never a man to commit himself till he knew whose opinion to agree with, Bob Cameron took intense interest in a pigeon on the balcony outside the office. Party president Ernie Watts looked at bagman Clarry Evans, who looked at Murdoch, who looked at Ben.

Simon got in first. "Great. Fantastic."

The suits beamed.

"You've cast the Government as the anti-Christ." Small had fixed the men from the agency with his finest steely look. "No," shrieked the fat suit. "When I said devil, I meant . . ."

"It is obvious what you meant. You are telling the voters, 'You think these guys are bad? The others may be even worse. Stick with the dull and boring morons who've screwed you because these other Flash Harrys are really tarts who will take you for an even bigger ride.'"

"It's inspirationally original, Simon," Ben maliciously threw in. "It may even be true."

"It is inspirationally awful, Ben." He snarled and he pulled off his gold-framed glasses, turning the full power of his frigid stare on the trio of suits. He took a deep breath and explained it as if he was addressing a group of pre-schoolers. "It is simple. This is a presidential-style campaign. The Prime Minister must be made to appear presidential. A statesman. A leader. The only leader of quality we have."

He paused. Murdoch nodded in appreciation. Cameron's earnest nod came a split second later.

Small paced the room and explained how the Prime Minister's vision must be shown and the Government portrayed as the only party that possessed such a broad perspective on the future. The other parties could be painted as bankrupt of ideas and backward looking. Small had a simple message for the Government to push in the run up to polling day.

"Yes, we have suffered. Yes, there has been pain. However, we are now about to get the payoff for all that hard work. Do not throw it away. That is what we tell the people and they will listen! Most of them have too much to lose, if only they knew it. Tell them what they have to lose and how easily it can be stripped away. Hit them where it hurts. Hit their fear."

The ad trio watched the other heads around the group nodding in unison and knew they were licked.

"If that's the brief, that's what you'll get," said the boss suit, hastily cranking up his enthusiasm levels. "It's more in the way of a refinement of what we were proposing. It's just we had to be sure how far you wanted us to go."

"Ad spend?" demanded Simon, in full control of the meeting now and enjoying it.

"Well," drawled Clarry, "Ernie will tell you the coffers are full. We are in a position to meet virtually any bills outside the funding granted by the Electoral Commission. We can produce *Ben Hur* if you want, although I hope you'll concentrate your spending on radio."

The ever diplomatic Cameron laughed dutifully at the State Radio Corporation chairman's joking pitch for the cash from the advertising revenue.

Nodding, Ernie Watts gave a quick sketch of the dire state of the party's once great electorate army. "Look, to be honest, I cannot do much more than put up the hoardings. Everything hinges on our advertising campaign. We just haven't the troops to put into the field that we had in the old days. The pension cuts, the arguments over Education, the Maori troubles, they all take a toll on supporters. Most branches tell us they haven't even got enough people to do a phone canvass of their electorates." The president shook his head and raised his voice over Murdoch's throat-clearing attempts to head off any criticism of the parliamentary wing's performance. "The problem is, Don, we have all this expensive computer gear designed to tell us where our support lies and who we should concentrate on getting off their bums to vote on the day, but the data to drive the system is missing. We are relying, in many cases, on canvassing information or phone checks that are three or four years old."

Murdoch was not a man to sit and listen to bad news when he could clutch at straws that might suggest better tidings. "Come on, Ernie. You have the focus groups. You have the rolling polls tracking every mood swing. We may not know exactly who they all are and how they'll vote individually, but we know exactly what they're thinking, what they want and what we have to say to them. You told me yourself at our last meeting." He was reddening with exasperation. "You told all of us that we had the most sophisticated polling system in the world. Hell, a goodly proportion of Clarry's hard-earned corporate money is going to feed your polling machine. It'd better work."

Ernie's small eyes narrowed even further and darted about for support that was entirely lacking from the men around him. "It's like this, Don. The polling tells us what people want us to do and we can then do it. We can even tell how they are reacting to our reaction. The polls tell us if we need more appeal with older voters, which we do. They tell us if we are not pulling well with women, which we aren't. We can see if you are an asset or a liability . . ." He trailed off for a second, realising he had dropped himself into deep water. "Ah, which, of course, Don, you are not. But we cannot hope to do what we did in the old days, which was isolate individual households that support us so we can knock on their doors on election day and haul their reluctant arses down to the polling station."

Ben's eyebrows shot up. Ernie Watts never swore. That convinced Ben, more than anything Watts had said, that the party was critically short of campaign foot soldiers.

Knowing Murdoch's need for soothing feedback, Simon cut in with news of the latest tracking polls that showed the Government was trending up and Cross's Freedom Party had peaked. Simon's tactics worked. Murdoch's obvious glee at that news took the sharp edges off his irritation with the now mute party president.

"Our focus groups" – Simon smiled and nodded at Ernie in an effort to bring him in from the cold to which Murdoch had consigned him – "are showing while they consider Cross 'honest', people are more dubious about the rest of his party. He runs a party of complete unknowns. People . . . and our people in the focus groups are no different . . . people fear the unknown. We have to feed that fear."

Ben thought that fear was justified. He had seen the rise and disintegration of many new parties. Most began with a few people who had a good idea. Within a very short time every disenchanted has been or loony who had ever been ejected from any other party had climbed on board the bandwagon and hijacked it. New parties were infested by flawed people looking for shortcuts to power or interest groups who rightly thought the new organisation could be useful to them. Generally new parties were the political equivalent of pyramid-selling scams. Those who were in first tended to be the smartest and most cunning while those that followed later were suckers. Or stupid. Or crooks. Maybe a combination of all three, he decided.

Meanwhile Simon Small was mercilessly gearing up to reiterate his hardline pitch for a heavily negative campaign in which the Freedom Party could be painted as closet Nazis and the rest of the Opposition line-up as quislings and fifth columnists. "If we stick to picking away at those fears raised by our focus group folk, we will screw Cross."

An unfortunate turn of phrase, Ben decided sourly, as he considered how Chris and his beloved Susan were at this moment probably spending their sordid lunchbreak. The thought plunged him into minor tailspin and he gazed out the windows towards the Hutt Valley as Small continued.

"Don't forget our target issues. We can't let someone like Cross drag us into simply defending the negatives like the Treaty settlement problems."

Murdoch coughed. "I don't see our approach to Treaty issues as a negative, Simon. If you recall our themes are reparation and reconciliation. How can this country go forward if it has still not reconciled its own past?" He was unconsciously quoting a keynote speech Ben had written for him months before.

On the subject of the Treaty the Prime Minister was an

enigma. His rural background suggested he should have followed the redneck prejudice of most of his party, which opposed cash and land settlements to Maori in settlement of century-old grievances. Instead, Murdoch pursued a determined path, against considerable internal party opposition, to the settlement process. Politically, his stance was pure masochism. Maori chastised him for moving too slowly while his enemies, like Cross, gleefully cashed in on a latently racist public mood that sullenly resented the reparations argument.

"Well, Prime Minister, such policy matters are, of course, your prerogative." Simon evaded any possibility of a clash, returning to his lecture on campaign style. "We have a range of pre-emptive strikes available to us on the positive side of the ledger. Health, for example. We have an entire advertising campaign, financed by the Health Department, that will highlight our increased targeted spending on Health. In particular, the 'Half the Waiting Time' scheme."

Murdoch raised an eyebrow, "Increased Health spending? Did I miss something? How did we get that one past Jane?"

"I said increased 'targeted' spending, Prime Minister. Not increased spending per se. We've found a little extra in the kitty." Small had their attention. "Simple really. We found we were spending an inordinate amount on drugs and surgical supplies. So, early last year, we simply changed the suppliers. We're now sourcing our products from a more competitively priced area of the market." He grinned and shook his head in despair. "These damn local health authorities just don't realise that medical supplies are not fashion items. You don't have to automatically buy from London, New York or Paris. We've found name brands able to source bulk surgical gear, blood products and a surprising array of drugs, from other more economical regions."

"Like where, Simon?" asked Bob Cameron. Ben decided either Bob was smarter than he appeared or had a well-honed survival instinct. Probably the latter.

"Regions with cheaper sources of labour, where major drug companies and pharmaceutical supply firms have set up manufacturing operations as foreign aid projects."

Cameron shrugged. "Third World."

"But first-class product," Simon stressed. "You would be amazed at the savings. With what we have managed to slice off the budget we can, gentlemen . . ." he paused for effect and met their eyes as he looked around. "We have accumulated enough from the Health vote to halve the waiting lists for non-acute care and totally eliminate any wait for more acute surgery."

There was an appreciative murmur around the room.

Dumb, Ben said to himself. Just plain dumb. Small and his tiny schemes were like top-dressing a prime piece of pasture with Claymore land mines. He dropped the damn things, everything looked fine, life continued as normal and then one day when you least expected it the lousy little things started going off and there were casualties everywhere. He reminded himself of Bradshaw's Rule Number One: if anything was likely to explode, it would explode during the campaign. His job was to clear a track through the minefield to polling day.

There was no point in directly tackling Small by pointing out he had placed the nation's sick in the leprous grasp of Third World health care. It was always best to avoid hand to hand combat in the Prime Minister's presence. Ben knew the best way to scuttle the plan was to take charge of the Officials Committee overseeing the Health scheme and wage a guerrilla campaign, slowly rolling it back by degrees. In the Beehive lasting success was, more often than not, achieved through trench warfare rather than blitzkrieg.

He made a mental note to organise an inter-departmental oversight committee, if there was not already one, and ensure he was chairman. Victory would not be easy: this was Small's pet project and the rest of the campaign committee were having small orgasms at the sheer simplicity of its machiavellian brilliance.

"Oh," Simon added with a smirk, "there is enough departmental money left for a highly effective advertising – sorry, public education – campaign promoting the message people now face 'Half the Waiting Time'. A slogan that says it all, really."

"Well done, Simon. Sounds like you've really got a handle on it." Murdoch became distracted as a rising level of argument outside his door became intrusive. Craning his neck in the direction of the racket, Murdoch dispatched Bradshaw to see what was happening.

Murdoch's two least favourite cabinet ministers stood, nose to nose, in the outer office that was the lair of the nervous little man known officially as the Prime Minister's personal private secretary. Almost purple with rage, Jane Street seemed to have puffed up to twice her already impressive size, a super-tanker bearing down on the small tugboat that was Stan Baker, known locally as the Minister for Rednecks.

He was, in fact, Associate Minister of Justice – a position held in tribute to his many years of undistinguished service as a solicitor in a small South Island law practice and, in that role, his undeniable ability to milk the legal aid system. Murdoch applied the old poacher-turned-gamekeeper principle to appoint Baker to the job. Stanley's first and only achievement as Associate Minister had been to plug the loopholes he had himself exploited so well, thus saving the Government a fortune in legal aid monies.

Sadly, at the moment, Stanley appeared to be in need of a good articulate defence counsel.

"You disgust me! You call yourself a Christian and you are nothing but filth!" she spat.

Baker flinched but stood his ground. "They were constituents," he blustered weakly. "Honestly, Jane . . ."

"Do you mistake me for an utter and complete fool, Stanley? How many of your constituents wear thigh-high boots and mini skirts and come calling at midnight? They were whores, Stanley!" she roared. "The Prime Minister will know this. I have had enough. He will know you for what you are, do you understand?"

Dear God, prayed Ben, it is a madhouse. Ronald, the timorous PPS, who had been frozen at his desk by the sheer venom of the spat, emitted a small squeak and fled. Through the open doors to the foyer Ben then saw press gallery veteran Daniel McGrath emerge from the lift and narrowly avoid being run down by the panic-stricken PPS.

"Oh great! McGrath!" breathed Ben.

It was McGrath who, years before in a disgracefully tabloid moment, had coined the term 'the Bantam Battler' for Stan Baker. Ben hastily slammed the door before the journalist could see him and tried to separate the pair.

Ben knew Baker was a brainless, vindictive, unscrupulous, xenophobic, morally corrupt, holier than thou bible basher, but also knew there was a wide streak of urban fascism in this country and that many loved him for his tough stands on law and order issues.

Right now the Bantam Battler was living up to his name, hissing at Street, "You miserable old bag. Just because you haven't had a leg-over since Adam was a little boy . . ."

"Ministers! Ministers! Please!" Ben wedged himself between them as Street bunched one meaty fist that she looked suspiciously ready to swing. "Stan, perhaps you could give me five minutes with Mrs Street. The PM is rather tied up at the moment and I see you're all a little stressed. Give me five minutes, I'll call you in your office."

"I was a lawyer in a highly successful country practice for years before you were born, sonny. I know slander when I hear it." Stanley was waving a pudgy finger under Ben's nose. "If that bitch spreads any of this I'll sue her fat arse off! And yours with it."

He swung abruptly on his heel with a snort of derision and barged out through the door, again almost flattening the unfortunate McGrath.

"Ben!" The reporter caught sight of Bradshaw, who was propelling Street behind him towards the internal circular corridor that ran around the ninth-floor offices.

"Not now, Danny, give me half an hour. I'll see you in the gallery," he said, slamming the door. Taking the still fuming Street by one of her hamhock arms, he marched her into his own outer office.

Peter, the suave older silver-haired press secretary, was leaning over the shoulder of Julie, who sat pecking at her word processor. Their bat-like ears had picked up every barb the ministerial pair had fired as they echoed around the circular corridor.

"Peter, why don't you check that McGrath's found his way to the lift."

"Righto!" Peter sprang to melodramatic attention and squeezed his way past the heaving Finance Minister.

Julie bit her lip to stifle a snigger. Glaring at her wide eyed, Ben pulled an imaginary zip across his lips and she smirked a nod in reply.

"All right." The door closed, Ben breathed a sigh of relief and the angrily flushed minister subsided into the sofa. "What on earth is going on, Mrs Street?"

"You know the Centrepoint apartments?" Jane Street demanded, her foghorn voice still redolent with disgust. Both Street and Baker had their ministerial flats in the luxury units and Mrs Street had the dubious pleasure of being on the floor below the Bantam.

Over the past three weeks, she explained, she had been wakened at midnight by young women ringing her doorbell demanding to see Stan Baker. The first few times she had redirected them to her neighbour upstairs but slowly it dawned on Street that there was something unusual about the nocturnal visits. The last time a pair of high-heeled shoes wobbled up to her door she had invited the woman in and discovered she was on a commercial errand.

"They are prostitutes, Ben. That poor creature told me Stan calls them over all the time and all of the girls hate it. He is, by all accounts, a thorough pervert! Worse, some of those girls didn't even look sixteen. The one I spoke to says he likes them as young as he can get."

Oh Lord, Ben groaned to himself. An election looming and we have a Cabinet Minister who likes to order late night take-aways of the Hugh Grant kind.

"Jane, I will sort this. Let me take it to the PM. He will know what to do." Ben cajoled her across the hall to the ministerial lift.

Back at his desk he looked at some notes he had hastily scribbled and picked up the phone. There was, in all probability, only one place Baker would be getting them from, Jack Bird's famous house of ill-repute in Oriental Bay.

"Jack, nice to hear your voice. How was the Iranian delegation last week? All behave themselves? Good. Look, I think we have a problem. I want a run-down, right now, on what Stan's been up to." He began scribbling.

It took Ben half an hour. He strode back through the central core of the Beehive and the receptionist paused in the middle of an argument with some unknown caller and their unfathomable grievance to wave an even fatter wad of phone messages.

"I'll get them on the way back, I promise," Ben lied.

Several minutes later the Prime Minister's door slammed behind the hunched retreating figure of Stan Baker and the air in the office began to clear.

"Where did you get these, Ben?" asked the Prime Minister, closing the plain brown manila folder. "Names, dates, times, money. It looks like you had twenty-four hour a day surveillance on Stan or the ladies."

"I don't think you really want to know all the details, boss. Jack Bird owes us a few favours. In fact, I think he thought he was doing us a favour sending Stan the girls. I must say, though, our Stan was a very busy boy."

Murdoch flicked the cover back for another quick look at the notes before passing it back across the desk with a quick snort of laughter, "Put it in that bottom drawer of yours, Benjamin, if there's any room left. I don't think think we'll need to use it. Stan has seen reason."

The contents of Ben's locked bottom drawer were legend in the building. While many thought the stories were apocryphal, they had labelled the mythical collection of political dirt the X-Files. Stan Baker had just joined the select few who had discovered to their cost that the fabled Bradshaw X-files really did exist.

If knowledge is power then Benjamin Bradshaw was the most powerful man in the country. He had read the story of the infamous FBI Chief J. Edgar Hoover and, while sternly disapproving of the way the man abused his office, Ben realised that you did not have to use such information to secure a hold over an opponent. Merely to possess it could be enough. Occasionally, however, when there was no other choice the file had to be pulled out of the drawer.

"Yes, Prime Minister." Ben enjoyed the moment of closeness the small victory had brought on. "You handled it pretty well. I thought he was going to cry when you read out the gory details. Amazing how many of them were called names like Chantelle and Cheri. Although I have to admit I am curious about Mistress Monique. I often wondered what they meant when they said Stan was a lay preacher. I guess now we know."

They both laughed. Murdoch enjoyed discovering others were even weaker than he.

"Ben, the whole damn thing is perfect. We could not have planned it better. For months he's been building up to quitting and joining either Cross or the bloody Christian Crusade Party. This has stymied him. He will go only when I tell him to," said Murdoch with satisfaction. "But I need the little swine with us for the moment. We cannot afford to have the Christians too strong yet. With Stan leading them they could easily suck six or seven percent off our party vote."

"They would be an ideal coalition partner after the election, boss."

"Imagine the power that would give the little shit. He'd be insufferable," Murdoch grunted. "No, he's safer and easier to control inside the cabinet. You keep that file handy, Ben, there will come a day of reckoning for Mr Stan bloody Baker, but not just yet."

"You'll be the one to tell Jane Street," said Ben drily.

"You leave the Battleaxe to me, Benny, leave her to me. She will just have to choke on her moral sensibilities for a while longer."

3

The Spin

The large airy bar at the Dockside on the waterfront was already full of testosterone-charged packs of young men in business suits and gaggles of pretty young women in short black dresses and smart red jackets.

It was curious to Ben that the mating rituals of the young middle class should be so obvious. The women dressed like huntresses, the men dragged the scent of their success across the bar-room floor. It was a meat market, he thought as he pressed through the crowd, but it was better than Bellamy's bar, where someone eavesdropped on every conversation and gossip was fuelled by every gesture you made.

He spied Susan leaning against the tall french doors looking out across the harbour, swathed in a long navy-blue wool coat, sipping her gin.

"It's my third and I'm rather enjoying it," she said dreamily, pecking him on the cheek.

"Dear Lord. Let me catch up," Ben laughed.

"My shout." Christopher Cross appeared beside them. "Scotch, Ben?"

"Thanks, Chris." Ben flicked a look at Susan, who blinked back at him innocently.

"I had no idea he would be here," she said.

Ben sighed theatrically. "I thought you had come to your senses and decided you couldn't live without me and here you are with another man."

"My only man, Ben," she emphasised, adding after a slight pause, "for the moment."

"He is not leaving Joyce for you?" Ben asked archly.

Susan levelled her gaze at him, the large brown eyes suddenly very hard. "I wouldn't want him to."

She did not look the femme fatale. Her pale face and the

dark curls falling across her forehead made her seem very vulnerable, and Ben wondered how much truth there was in her insistence that the affair with Chris was nothing more than an idle dalliance. Ben had spent enough years in the capital to know the life of a Wellington mistress could be a harsh one. The political mistress absorbed a certain measure of power and prestige by osmosis but she was inevitably excluded from the public side of her lover's life, condemned to the shadows of the evening and a few snatched hours in soulless flats like Chris's tiny apartment in Molesworth Street.

Cross returned with more drinks, ignoring the heads that turned to follow him and the occasional ironic cheer from the other side of the bar. He was instantly recognisable, tall, blond, tanned and athletic. Ben sourly noted Chris seemed not to have added even a kilo since their university days together. He was a smooth bastard then and he was even slicker now.

With the intuitive ability to go for the jugular that had put him in serious contention for the top slot in politics, Cross reached out and patted Ben's stomach. "Whoa! You put on a few pounds, Buddy?" Chris said. "Too many of those Rotary Club dinner speeches. Hot chicken and curry and rice. Jesus, you think they'd vary the menu. I told my people I am not going to talk to another service club unless they're serving something healthier than that crap. Of course," he bellowed at Ben over the roar of the bar crowd, "if you have to sit there and listen to Murdoch babble on, I wonder you can even eat."

Ben counted sourly to himself. Two digs at me in twenty seconds. Unconsciously he sucked his stomach in a little as Cross carried on.

"Never mind the election result, bud, you can still have a job with me. Murdoch doesn't deserve you!" Cross's mouth was barely an inch from Ben's ear.

"Yeah, yeah, would you buy a used Government off this man?" He gestured at Cross.

Grinning over her drink, Susan watched the pair going through their sparring ritual. It had been the same ever since she had known them. Both men were enormously competitive and, at times, the friction between them was obvious. They appeared to be total opposites: Chris tall and good looking in an Aryan way with his white-blond hair, Ben mousier, balder, shorter and rounder in a middle-aged Kiwi way. Susan smiled to herself. Chris must use half a can of spray or a litre of gel to get his hair that securely held in place; if Ben were ever confronted with a tube of gel he would assume it was some kind of marital aid. Chris had an obsession with plain blue, crisply pressed, single-breasted triple-button suits bought from his favourite tailor off London's Oxford Street. Very *GQ* or *Fashion Quarterly*. Ben, by contrast, could make Hugo Boss look like a Salvation Army store reject. His business suits began life as highly priced, skilfully cut garments. Within seconds of touching his bulky body they had sagged into chunks of hideously creased linen.

They could not be more different. Yet both men shared a kind of vital energy. It was easy to see what women of all ages found alluring about Cross – undeniably he had classic good looks – but Ben had never been accused of being handsome. It was the quality of his mind that drew certain women to him. Susan conceded that what he lacked in looks he made up for in wit. Chris, burdened with the vanity common to all politicians, was inclined to take himself far too seriously. Ben Bradshaw took very little seriously. He earnestly sweet-talked women into bed seducing women with laughter and cheeky persistence.

Chris turned away to shout a greeting to someone behind them and Susan leaned across to whisper in Ben's ear, "How many women have you joked into bed?" She giggled.

Ben stared at her, grinning in return. "What on earth brought that on?"

"I have no idea. I think this had better be my last drink."

"Hmmm. Have another. Maybe tonight we can finally get to the punchline, Ms Lewis?" His eyebrows raised in mock lechery.

Laughing, Susan lightly punched him on the arm as he began a parody of her own coy eyelid-batting technique.

"Hey, Speedy! " A large florid man elbowed his way through the crowd toward Chris, who twisted around in irritation at the call.

"Uh-oh!" murmured Ben.

"What's the matter?" said Susan, suddenly aware that Chris's hackles had risen.

"At university Chris was known as Speedy."

"Why?" she asked.

"Some said it was because of the pace he showed as a winger. Others say it came from a rather public complaint made by a girlfriend at the time."

Cross was applying the freeze to his long-lost ruddy-faced university friend and within a few minutes he drifted back into their corner. The intruder drunkenly lurched back to his own group and could be heard loudly declaiming how snobby Cross had become.

"Don't you hate it when these characters come out of the woodwork after all these years," Chris snapped.

Ben nodded. He vaguely recognised the florid-faced man from the varsity rugby club in the seventies, and the two men spent several minutes trying to work out who he was. Eventually they decided he was not worth knowing then or now.

Ben snapped his fingers. "He used to date Melissa the Kisser."

"I remember her. Hell, I used to date her," said Chris.

"I know. You stole her off me at the Kiwi after pub crawl one year. I think she was the one that gave you the nickname."

"Hold on. Don't get shirty with me, Bradshaw. As I recall you had stolen Melissa off that oaf not long before."

"That doesn't count. I was in love with her."

Chris laughed. "Was there ever a woman you weren't in raptures over?"

"Jane Street," Ben fired back and they both roared with laughter.

Susan marvelled how two men who had been chipping away at each other just a short time before could turn around so quickly and become allies when confronted with a common enemy. If that was how their friendship got its strength, she thought, then it was about to be forged in bonds of steel by the next arrival. Daniel McGrath was pushing through the throng towards them, oblivious to the trail of spilt drinks and angry mutterings from those who were too near his flailing elbows.

"Oh shit," the trio chorused.

It was not that they disliked McGrath. He could be hilariously funny in a bitchy way. He had a klaxon for a voice and an extensive repertoire of political gossip that he animatedly relayed at enormous volume to anyone within a one-hundred-metre radius. However, prolonged exposure to McGrath could be injurious to your hearing, your liver, your wallet and your reputation.

"Well! What a cosy little group! The biggest thorn in Murdoch's side having a quiet drink with Murdoch's favourite spin-doctor," he drawled. "And the lovely Sue playing gooseberry."

All three could see the wheels churning as McGrath tried to figure out exactly who was doing what with whom.

Ben felt Susan lean her body against him and slip her arm through his. McGrath's eyes flickered for an instant, taking in the gesture. Great, thought Ben, it will be all round the gallery tomorrow that I am bonking her. Of course, that was exactly what Ben Bradshaw would have liked to be doing but to be publicly outed without having had the luck to have consummated the affair would be extremely annoying. Damn Susan, he decided, for making him her camouflage.

The gossip had already been filed away in McGrath's encyclopaedic brain and he had skipped on to meatier issues. He zeroed in on Cross, demanding to know what had happened to Stan Baker. "One minute he's all set to jump ship from the Government to you or the God Botherers, the next minute he's gone quiet. Not a peep out of him. Something's happened." He turned to Ben. "You wouldn't happen to know what the Minister for Rednecks is up to, would you? Bradshaw, old boy?"

Danny McGrath, who had been dragged up on the wrong side of the tracks in Onehunga, had nevertheless acquired the annoying private-school habit of using people's surnames in a way that leant a patronising emphasis to everything he honked.

"Ah, well, McGrath. While a true Christian to the core," Ben replied, "Stanley is a loyal member of the Government and the Conservative Party. He is a dead cert to become Attorney-General after the election. A man with a great future before him in the Thousand Year Reich of the Murdoch administration." Ben had lapsed into his best defensive strategy. Reporters found it disarming when he seemed even more cynical about his employers than they were.

McGrath shouted with laughter. "Bullshit! The fact is he might be about to leap the other way onto the Cross bandwagon. Chris?"

"I don't think so, Danny. It is true that we are sharing a stage in my electorate next week to discuss law and order issues. In fact, he will even be staying at my place. We are old friends – as you know we flatted together when we were backbenchers but do not, I repeat, McGrath, do *not* start running speculative stories that he is coming over to the Freedom Party. He's not."

"I can tell you categorically, Danny," he continued. "Stan Baker will not become a member of my party. Full stop. Exclamation mark. Banner headline reads 'Cross Rules out Baker'. Got it?"

"Thank you, Chris. I can write my own stories." McGrath seemed miffed to have lost a good yarn before it had even got off the ground. "Well, tell me then, why is he suddenly so quiet? Why no announcement he is going off on a mission from God?"

"He's seen the error of his ways, Danny," said Ben. "Who knows why Stanley Baker does anything? He's a Southlander. You know what they're like in Invercargill. The cold and damp rot their brains. Forget it, there are more important things happening."

Daniel McGrath's mind was sharp but it seemed capable of having only one thought in it at a time. The question of Stan Baker was instantly erased as Ben drew him aside to give him a preview of the Government's Health initiatives due out the following week.

It was more than a simple distraction. Ben figured by tipping McGrath to a few of the potentially controversial aspects of the new policy package he could use the unsourced news story that would inevitably follow to fly a few kites. If there was a vitriolic public response to any of the proposals the Government could amend them, deny them, or massage public opinion before the Health strategy was officially announced.

McGrath knew he was being used, but this was part of the symbiotic relationship between the Government and the gallery. Danny got a story, Ben got to check out all the pitfalls and road-test a tricky issue before the Government became welded to it as policy.

Bored at being left out of whatever McGrath and Ben were discussing and wary of being seen to have too intimate a conversation with Susan in the crowded bar, Chris was getting restless.

"Where are we going to dinner, folks?" he demanded.

Ben noticed a flash of hurt in Susan's eyes. No quiet dinner for two. Chris wanted to play with the boys. No boats in harbours tonight, he thought with more than a little satisfaction. When Chris went out to play no one got home before three in the morning.

"Paradiso?" ventured Ben.

"Hasn't been the same since they had the fire," said Susan. Her negativity was unlikely to divert Cross from a good night out.

"What about Il Casino?" Chris suggested.

"Only if the Freedom Party is paying," said Ben, watching McGrath squirm awkwardly. It was a journalist's nightmare to be caught between the prospect of losing either a free meal or an exclusive story. Ben was curious to see how he would solve the dilemma of getting the article written but still manage to go out on the town.

"Have another drink first," McGrath said, pulling a small black mobile phone from his pocket, "and I'll join you after I make a quick call." He disappeared out onto the veranda over the water and could be seen with a finger in one ear yelling into the phone.

"Is he talking to the unfortunate Mrs McGrath?" asked Susan as she peered out into the night where McGrath paced, gesticulating wildly.

"Don't be silly, he'd never call her. He's filing his story down the phone to a copytaker," chuckled Chris as he thrust another drink into her hand.

"You gave him a story!" Susan angrily turned on Ben. "What did you tell him?"

Laughing, Ben choked on his scotch. "It's all right, I'll talk to you about it later. You'll have it for the morning. All you'll have to do is be fresh enough to get up and get into the newsroom before seven."

Susan fumed, knowing her night would now have to end a lot earlier than her lover's would. "You bastard. I know what you're doing."

"You want the yarn or not? Of course you do. Never look a gift story in the mouth." Ben smiled and turned up the volume on his charm. "I'll make sure you have details Daniel doesn't have. I kept the best of it for you. In fact, he'll be spitting when he turns on the radio in the morning."

Susan looked a little mollified.

Cross shook his head, whispering, "You really will have to work for me when we win, Ben. Awesome to watch. You are slick, bud."

"Never happen, Chris. Murdoch will not have you within a bull's roar of the Cabinet table and you know you can't get anything like a majority in your own right."

"Wait, Ben. Wait and watch."

Cross was way too smug for Ben's comfort. He made a mental note to call the gophers he had sent off to check the Freedom Party backdoor funding deal Susan had mentioned at their last meeting. There had to be a money trail they could follow. If Chris Cross was this cocky he must have a full war chest, and the only way he could have got that level of funding was through big business.

He teased Cross, saying it took more than cake stalls and raffles to fund a campaign and there was not a businessman in the country would give him the time of day after the Fund affair.

The trick worked. Mention the Dominion Super-annuation Fund to Christopher Cross and all reason went out the window.

"You know they're shysters, Ben. They're crooks and I can prove it. Hell, I have proved it in the House, day after day. How much more bloody evidence do they need to have a public inquiry?"

Bradshaw wisely remained quiet as Cross went on, "They pillaged that fund. A public fund, a state asset. The men your Government appointed to the board of that company went in and ruthlessly used other people's savings, other people's insurance money and retirement funds to shore up their own shonky investments. They ran the

Dominion Superannuation Fund into the ground to the point where the taxpayer had to bail them out."

Part of the bar crowd had fallen silent. They were witnessing, live in the flesh, what they had previously only seen on TV, a fiery Chris Cross coming out all guns blazing.

"Everyone lost, Ben. The taxpayers. The investors. The old people who were counting on that money for their retirement years. Everyone lost except the Dirty Dozen," he said, referring to the directors of the Fund. All were big businessmen. All twelve were extremely rich and well known as big financial backers of the Government. "They're as guilty as sin and I will get that public inquiry, Ben. You and your Don Murdoch will not stop me either."

He was right on both counts, Ben mused. The Dirty Dozen were crooks and there would be a public inquiry. Not till after the election though and, even then, it would be difficult to pin these men. The Dirty Dozen had not become obscenely rich without learning to cover their tracks well.

Cross could speculate and fire wild accusations from within the sanctuary of Parliament but it was quite another matter to prove the case against the Fund's directors before a judge in a formal Commission of Inquiry. All the vital evidence against the directors would have long since passed through the shredder. Any of the Fund's share purchases that might have coincided with the directors' own personal holdings could be passed off as sheer coincidence. After all, Ben could hear the defence lawyers claim, rich men have large, diverse share holdings. There will inevitably be some correspondence in their personal investments and the prudent distribution of equities within a large public corporation like the Dominion Super-annuation Fund. To put it more succinctly, the lawyers would be saying, "Prove it," and Cross would find it hard to oblige.

"Right! Which restaurant are we going to?" McGrath yelled over the noise of the bar.

"Do you ever type a story yourself, Danny?" asked Ben.

"He can't type," smiled Chris. "He just bellows what he imagines to be the facts and someone else turns it into English."

"Ha bloody ha! I'll have you know I can write like a dream," said McGrath haughtily.

"You write *in* a dream, Danny," Susan groaned. "Let's eat. Il Casino wins."

Chris had a swagger to his stride as he strolled through the Dockside bar, nodding and smiling as greetings flew. He stiffened slightly as he passed a group in the corner by the window.

"Luke."

"Chris." A good-looking Maori man in his early forties gave him a mock salute and turned to attend more effusively on Ben. "Bwana! Good to see you down here with the peasants. Us humble blackfellas don't see guys like you that often these days. Unless you have some more blankets and muskets you want to trade."

Luke Watene was the Freedom Party's candidate for Eastern Maori. He might even take the seat, according to the latest internal party poll figures. Luke was once a radical, would still like to pretend he was, but he had taken too large a role in the Treaty settlement process not to have become decidedly more middle of the road.

"Nice duds, Luke," said Ben as he sped past, reaching down and fingering the lapel of Watene's suit. "A Hugo Boss blanket or maybe Zegna?"

The other Maori at the table laughed caustically and so did Watene himself.

The twin doors swung shut behind the departing group and Cross turned back to Ben.

"By the way, don't think I was fooled by that little smokescreen you put up over Stan Baker. You've been up to something, buddy. You or that clod you call a boss. I must have a word to Stan when he's up at my place next weekend. It could prove interesting."

Interesting? Bloody fascinating if Stan spilled his guts, thought Ben. Yet he could not imagine how Baker, even with the aid of a medicinal sherry after an evening thumping his favourite themes of law and order and family values could reveal to Cross that he spent his otherwise lonely nights in the capital ordering hot and cold running hookers.

"Let me know what you find out, Chris. I'll be just as interested as you are."

Cross's eyes twinkled with amusement at the game.

4
The Spin

"I will not have him, Simon. I will not have him." Murdoch held firm. "It's not just a matter of whatever bad blood there may be between us. The money markets will not tolerate him. The economy is simply too fragile."

The Prime Minister stood up and paced across the kitchen floor as the band in the hall struck up the 'Tennessee Waltz'.

"It's late if they're playing that," he muttered. "It's getting late for us, too. The markets are still open on the other side of the world. They'll be selling Kiwi like it's yesterday's shit paper. You understand, Simon?"

Small straightened and looked away from Murdoch's glare.

"If I take that bodgie Cross on board, they'll crucify us. Hell, Simon, you were the one that sold us to the electorate saying, 'It's us or chaos.' Wasn't that your message, boy? Well, I'll tell you what. You've created a . . . what do you call it, Ben? A self-fulfilling prophecy. We try a coalition with the damn lunatic Freedom Party and the whole house of cards collapses. I'm talking a crash that will make '87 look like fun times. No. No. No! Cross is out and he stays out."

He slumped back into his seat and poured himself another scotch. Ben reached over and grabbed the bottle. "I'll join you, boss".

Faith tutted quietly but smiled. Small simply screwed his lips in a tight pucker and stalked towards the door.

"I'll make a few calls."

"You do that, Simon," called Ben as the Diplomatic Protection Squad officer outside slid the door closed behind Small. It opened a second later and Tony the DPS policeman popped his head back to announce that the media had been giving him a hard time about getting a press conference but

Small's exit through the mob had proved an excellent diversion. The entire pack moved like a tide through the hall, scattering the dancers, following Simon as he tried to get some privacy to use his phone.

"If they come back, tell them to bugger off," barked Murdoch. The security man smiled, giving him the thumbs up as he closed the door.

"I've got the giggles," sniggered Ben. "The hacks will stick to Simon like glue. He won't even be able to go to the urinal without worrying if Danny McGrath is hiding in the cistern."

Murdoch laughed. "Knowing McGrath, he probably is."

They both cackled quietly for a while. It may have been the scotch. It may just have been the relief from the pressure of a five-week election campaign and the stress of the months that preceded it, but the men had struck a chord for the first time since their first landslide win many years before.

"Benny, I've buggered it up. I know that. I let too many other people have their way. I knew what I wanted and what I should be doing. I didn't follow my instincts." In a rare moment of generosity he added, "I didn't listen to you."

Dear Lord, thought Ben, he is becoming a brooding drunk and it is far too early in the evening for that. It was time to fight back.

"Come on, boss. Let's canvass the options." He used the phrase he always used to try and focus Murdoch on a particular issue and again the ploy worked.

"Options, Ben. Options. There are always options," the Prime Minister groaned, leaning across the table. "Let me have 'em."

"Option one, we deal with Richard Foot. We're talking a

Conservative-Liberal coalition. "If it comes to a scrap in the House, Foot's Liberals give you enough seats to outnumber both the Freedom Party and the Socialists." Ben paused as Murdoch screwed up his nose.

"I've thought about this one, Ben. It won't work."

"Why not?" Ben insisted. Why break the habit of a lifetime and start thinking now, he added to himself. "You can work with the Liberals. OK, you'll have to ease up on labour laws a little. You might have to spend a little more on social services but really, boss, you can deal with this guy."

"Foot is a lunatic," said Murdoch despairingly.

"Since when has that been an impediment to holding high office?" snorted Ben. "I'm dialling Foot's headquarters on the land line. Let's hear what he has to say."

The Liberal leader was waiting by the phone. "Benny! Good to hear your voice. So, Murdoch's ringing to concede, eh?"

"Those times are long gone, Dick," said Ben. "With MMP we can all be winners, if we strike the right deal."

He could hear Foot laughing and the fencing continued with Foot offering to take the Conservatives into a Government led by the Liberals.

Ben sniped back that, perhaps, the Conservatives might allow him a seat in Cabinet if the Liberals entered a formal coalition as junior partner.

"Benny! That's not an offer. That's an insult. I think I hear Chris Cross on the other line."

"What's your price, Dick? Cards on the table."

"I don't want to talk to the monkey, put the organ grinder on the line," Foot snapped.

Ben placed his hand over the receiver and said, "I think he's about to do us a deal but he wants to make it with you."

Murdoch grunted and took the phone. Several more grunts followed before he hung up.

Faith and Ben stared at him.

"No deal," Murdoch snapped.

Foot's price was too high; the role of Deputy Prime Minister, nine key Cabinet portfolios and a host of policy U-turns that included a complete restructuring of the country's labour laws.

"I'm not selling out to the damn unions. They already have Foot by the short and curlies. They're not getting me by proxy." Murdoch, a farmer, had little but scorn for the trade unions. Working his way up the ladder in successive Conservative Governments, he had constantly come into conflict with obstinate unions in almost every portfolio he held. Although, to be fair, he and the grizzled old-breed unionists had often found common ground in the all-night drinking bouts in his Beehive office that followed the settlement of some protracted dispute. However, the old guard out of the pragmatic Tom Skinner and Jim Knox mould were fast disappearing, to be replaced by younger, more narrow-minded men and women almost indistinguishable from the dour Treasury and State Services officials that confronted them across the table.

The Cold War doctrine of the Knoxes and Skinners at least gave them some backbone. These new dapper little men with briefcases were nothing but accountants with a conscience.

Ben interrupted his train of thought. "Foot, Prime Minister?"

"Bugger Foot."

"Not a preferred option, thank you, Prime Minister. To return to the subject at hand. Everything Richard Foot demands is negotiable," Ben suggested.

"Maybe. But there is the question of Health. Foot is adamant he wants the Health portfolio. It is central to their entire strategy. Sadly, Ben, I don't think we can let him near the Ministry's files, can we?"

"Oh. I see what you mean."

Faith pulled a chair up to the table and for the first time took an active role in the proceedings.

"Don, what do you mean you can't let him near the Health files?"

"Darling, it's nothing. Just a small skeleton or two lurking there. A bit of an embarrassment. If it comes out, the Government will not look great, and I would rather not play Russian roulette by giving Foot access to that kind of ammunition."

She was looking very attentively at her husband as she asked, "What exactly was the problem, Don? What skeleton?"

He shuffled anxiously. "I don't want you worried about this kind of stuff, Faith. Besides, I've said it before and I'll say it again. Foot is mad."

Seeing Murdoch was trying to avoid giving Faith any specifics of the political scandal that lay beneath the surface of the Health Department, Ben quickly stepped in and helped change the subject. It was habit born of years of bailing his boss out of similar situations.

"Shall I call Danny McGrath in and get his opinion on whether we take Foot?" he joked.

Murdoch cackled, knowing the story but enjoying the prospect of having it retold to Faith. Somehow gossip tinged with scandal always made him feel more virtuous, especially when it concerned a rival.

"Danny and Dick Foot had a bit of a falling out in

Shanghai," Ben explained to Faith, who blinked back at him uncomprehendingly.

"A major falling out," laughed Murdoch. "Falling out of the bus! The question is, who got shanghaied." This was the closest Murdoch could get to wit.

"It was when Foot was on an official tour of China. They had been on the delegation's bus for hours coming back from a factory visit in some God awful place way out in the countryside. Dick was up front boring his business buddies. His wife Dawn was down the back . . . uh . . ." Ben faltered under Faith's attentive gaze.

"Dawn was down the back doing her own boring with the journos," Murdoch bellowed. "If you know what I mean, Faith."

She did not.

"Well, boss, she wasn't . . . you know . . . uh . . . having it off with him," Ben faltered.

"Danny McGrath had his hand up her skirt," roared Murdoch.

"Oh." Faith was caught between astonishment and horrified curiosity.

"It was dark. She and Danny had been drinking. The bus trip had been grinding on for hours. They just got a little frisky." Telling such a tawdry story to someone as naive as Faith Murdoch made Ben feel like he needed his mouth washed out with soap.

"Frisky? She had been giving him a leg-over all the trip, you told me," Murdoch demanded.

"Well, PM, I've got no evidence of that. Anyway," he said hastily, trying to finish the sad tale and get on with the night's business, "Dick sussed something was wrong and eased his way down the bus. They were too busy snogging and never noticed. He whipped off the blanket they had thrown over themselves and there was McGrath looking like the original one-armed bandit. Dick got in a couple of good shots to McGrath's head before the DPS cop separated them."

Murdoch laughed, slapping the table hard. He enjoyed the story more every time it was told.

"I always knew that woman was common," Faith sniffed and picked up the huge teapot.

"Dawn Foot? Common? What about McGrath?" Murdoch asked, round eyed.

"Daniel McGrath can't help himself. Men can't. She should have known better," she called over her shoulder as she struggled out with the teapot.

Like a cow cocky working a stock gate the policeman deftly slid the door far enough aside to allow Faith through into the crowded hall before jerking it closed to head off the rush by the media mob who had obviously abandoned the chase with Simon Small. Ben caught sight of McGrath's frantically bobbing head trying to attract his attention before the door shut.

"What does she mean, men can't help themselves? I've never strayed," Don Murdoch blustered, slightly annoyed that his teasing attempt to shock his wife had failed, once again.

"I think she means we all easily succumb to one temptation or another, Prime Minister. While we're on the subject, I'll have another of those." He gestured with an empty glass to the bottle.

"I see what you mean about Foot and the Health Ministry though." Ben nodded his thanks for the drink. "If he tumbled to the surgical supply cock up, we would be dead meat. You know now Simon thinks there is some criminal liability involved in that fiasco. That the liability goes all the way to the top."

"Not me," said Murdoch. "The buck stops with Jane Street and that dopey bugger I was dumb enough to let her talk me into making Minister of Health."

"Ah. Well. I think you'll find she was cunning enough to put the surgical supply deal before Cabinet and have the decision minuted."

"Jesus." Shaking his head, Murdoch moaned in quiet despair. "When did she do that? I can't remember that decision going through. She probably did though. I wouldn't have noticed it. She talks in bureaucratic gobbledygook most of the time."

"Small insists there was a Cabinet minute. That makes you all liable," Ben drawled. He liked seeing Don's well-armoured self-confidence take a dent or two. "Still, no use worrying about it now. We've got bigger fish to fry. What's the risk Foot will tango with Cross and maybe the Socialists? They could cut us out altogether and form their own Government."

The pair discussed the prospect briefly before deciding a three-way coalition could not last longer than the meeting that tried to put it together. The opposition parties were too deeply divided. It would be political suicide for the left-wing Socialists to be tied into a Cabinet dominated by the milder social democrats of the Liberal Party and the crazy populists of the Freedom Party. The left would be hopelessly compromised by association with the others and its fragile support would wither and disappear in disgust.

Simon Small bustled back still clutching his mobile phone to his ear.

"He won't listen to me. You tell him," he cried, holding out the phone to Murdoch.

"Who is it?" snapped Murdoch.

"Jane Street. Talk to her."

"Not on that phone, Simon." Ben held up a hand in warning.

"Not on any phone, Simon," said the Prime Minister. "Tell her I'll call her in the morning. I'm a bit tied up right now."

Small exhaled dramatically and stalked to the other side of the kitchen mumbling into the phone before snapping it shut with a dramatic slap.

"If you won't listen to reason, will you at least tell me what you propose to do?" he demanded.

"All in the fullness of time, Simon. All in the fullness of time."

Murdoch specialised in infuriating those he thought he could annoy with impunity. Yet he inflicted little real hurt, just minor pinpricks to the vanity of self-important people, and he could occasionally display real kindness.

A few months before, Ben had chaired a committee meeting on one of his pet projects, coordinating the public relations and advertising strategies of most of the Government departments.

For years these organisations had spent millions of dollars promoting their respective wares on Welfare, Education, Health, Housing, Tourism, Conservation, Police and all the many varied functions of government. It was Ben's theory that these disparate campaigns could be welded together with a common theme that might advantage the Murdoch Government in the coming campaign. Not that he would be so obvious in his approach, after all, the Auditor-General's office would be watching for any sign that public money might be spent for party political purposes.

"Remember," Ben told the sceptical men and women around the long timber table. "This is about making publicly owned services and benefits more freely available to the people. It's about demystifying the apparatus of state, empowering people so they can feel freer about taking advantage of what is rightfully theirs."

The committee looked no less sceptical than before, but at least they were not heckling.

"Hence we are talking about the Working for You programme. Put quite simply, wherever possible and pratical all publicly funded advertising carries the words 'Working for You' on the end. Newspapers, magazines, radio and television. A common theme. A common logo. We knit it all together and run a parallel campaign promoting the concept that the agencies of state are there 'Working for You'."

One of the public relations women from the Department of the Environment raised her hand. She explained this might work where organisations like, say, Social Welfare were pushing a range of benefit changes, but what about corporate profile advertising that simply sought to improve the image of the department or to remind the public that it existed?

"I'm glad you raised that, " he responded, making a mental note to check and see how long her contract had left to run. "In fact, any image campaign is ideally suited to Working for You. Take for example the Department of the Environment. You can run all the nice nature commercials you want and at the end you stress that the Department is 'Working for You'.

"It is important that people feel they are getting value for their tax dollars. This project will ensure that. Now, as you are aware, we are establishing an inter-departmental oversight committee which will need to see and give final approval to any campaigns you are planning from this time on. I look forward to our next meeting."

The committee members dispersed, exchanging looks of mutual annoyance at the encroachment by the Beehive powers that be on their respective territory. The PR barons in each department enjoyed their independence and the power it gave them.

If there was no such thing as a free lunch, no one had told the advertising industry, which plied them with food and entertainment. After all, these bureaucrats controlled many millions of advertising dollars. A temporary economic recession might see the commercial sector rein in their advertising budgets but the state usually increased its spending during hard times. In an agency a Government account was to be treasured and guarded jealously, although the agency executives who ran such accounts always loathed the time-wasting, timidity and conservatism of their state clients.

Peter, the PM's senior press secretary waited behind, rocking to and fro, as Ben collected his papers from the table.

"What's up, Peter?"

"Who am I? What am I doing here?" Peter liked to pretend he was far vaguer than he really was and the line had become an old joke between them. "Oh, yes. Ben. Ah . . . remember Harry."

Ben remembered Harry, his predecessor.

"Well, it seems he has a few financial problems since he left. Nothing serious but . . . ah . . . he needs a job."

"He can't have mine back," said Ben.

"Noooo! Never. No. Just a small board or committee perhaps. Something that will put a few more badly needed dollars in his pocket. He really needs it. The divorce wiped him out." Peter stood looking at the ceiling while he made his pitch.

Ben sighed. "I'll talk to the PM about it."

Much to Ben's surprise, Murdoch leapt to help Harry, whose departure from the ranks of the PM's office was not exactly on the best of terms. Harry had been a close confidant of Murdoch's predecessor.

"The Pest Control Board," said Murdoch. "Give him a seat on the Pest Control Board. They don't meet a lot and when they do it's always somewhere different, so he'll make a bit on the travel expenses if he's crafty."

"Pest Board?" Ben was flummoxed.

"Just the thing," Murdoch replied. "They're always zipping about catching foreign bugs and butterflies and worms and snakes and things. He'll enjoy it. Besides, sounds like the poor bugger needs every cent he can get. Do me a memo to the Minister in charge. He'll sort it out. Might even make him chairman."

Murdoch was capable of random acts of kindness, which was more than could be said for some of his rivals.

5
The Spin

S usan buried her face deep into his shoulder. The worst
of the storm had passed but small waves of sobs would
still wrack her body and he held her closer.

The scene contained elements of one of Ben's favourite
fantasies. He had dreamed Cross eventually would commit
one emotional atrocity too many and it would fall to Ben to
provide Susan with the comfort and support she needed. The
fire would flicker in the living room of his Wadestown house,
they would nestle on the couch, her warm breath on his
neck, and gradually she would realise the extent of her
mistake in spurning him.

What he had not taken into account was her very real
pain. Her anguish at Chris's latest betrayal pierced him
almost as much as her.

Susan appeared on his doorstep just after eleven and
she stood at the window, staring silently down at the
harbour for nearly a hour before she spoke. Ben had poured
her a drink and another for himself as she began to talk.

Like everything with Cross, she told him, nothing was
clear cut. Chris wanted to put their relationship on hold. The
campaign was looming closer. He had powerful enemies. He
thought he was being watched. There was too much to lose
in a scandal. The party depended on him. He could lose his
children. Susan's reputation and her job were also at risk.
She noted she had been added as an after-thought.

Susan had waited for the real reason. When Chris fell
quiet she felt a cold calm come over her and she began a
cross-examination that would have done credit to a
barrister. She sensed him squirm as she demanded, why
now? Their relationship had been an open secret around the
capital for months and he had not worried. Only last Friday
they had spent the morning in bed together and he had

promised he would leave his wife after the election was over. What had happened?

There was no answer. He stood with his face averted and she realised it was not with shame. There was a graze on his cheekbone and the flesh around his right eye was distinctly discoloured. Who had he been fighting with?

"It's all the fault of that little shit, Stan Baker, Ben," she later explained to Ben.

The law and order forum in Cross's electorate had proved a great success but Baker's stay as a house guest was a rank disaster. Chris had a short attention span and Stan's carping sanctimoniousness wore him down as they sat in his lounge late into the night. Joyce Cross dutifully showed Baker the courtesy of her attention and Chris decided to go to bed. Stan would be content with an audience of one.

"That was his mistake, Benny. Leaving the two of them alone." Susan turned from the window and went on.

When Cross went to bed Stan felt free to praise him as a great man, wonderful leader, fantastic politician. But, Baker told Joyce, Chris was flawed. Like all great men, Chris had great flaws. He suggested they pray for him.

Joyce went to church only occasionally but, despite her embarrassment, she knelt beside Stan Baker on the carpet. It took her a second or two to realise what Stan was actually intoning in his best Baptist revivalist tones.

Susan recounted what happened next, playing the roles of both Joyce and Stan.

"What did you just say, Stan?"

"I said, Mrs Cross, your husband is a man who faces many temptations and it is only human that he should succumb on occasion. May we, as the Lord does, forgive Christopher his infidelity. May God help him to stop his adultery. And, Lord, we pray for forgiveness for the sins of that woman Lewis who brazenly seduced him."

Apparently Joyce did not wait to say amen. Most of Chris's bruising was to his torso, although she had managed to land at least two solid punches to his head and a knee to his groin before he was fully awake and able to flee.

Cross spent the night in a motel down on the foreshore, a kilometre from his home, listening to Stan's stuttered apologies. Joyce's final act had been to evict her unwanted lodger. It was hard for Chris to know which was worse, Joyce throwing him out or ending up having a sleepless night listening to Baker's pious drivel.

Hearing all this, Ben sat on the couch biting his lip.

"Such is the power of prayer, dear," he said softly.

Susan's shoulders began to heave. He realised she was laughing but it did not last long. As she slumped onto the couch beside him she began to quietly cry and as time went on the sobs became great cries of pain.

He was still thinking about it the next morning as he leafed through a file of papers in the back of the limousine. The difference between fantasy and reality was tears, he decided. In his daydreams Susan lay in his arms, her faced upturned, their eyes locked. In that instant he would murmur exactly the right words, her face would light up with recognition of the inevitability of it all and their very hot steamy future would be sealed with a smouldering kiss.

Instead, her face had stayed buried in his shoulder soaking his shirt with her tears until she finally fell asleep. Eventually, he had gently laid her back on the couch, pulled a rug over her, closed the curtains and gone to bed. Alone.

She had left by the time he awoke. He even missed the chance of a secondary seduction attempt with his universally acclaimed breakfast special, Eggs Benedict. Whoever said the way to a man's heart was through his stomach had their genders wrong. Most of the women Ben knew had a love/hate relationship with food. They might periodically deny themselves meals for reasons of fashion but they still held a passionate regard for it. He once flatted with a chef who insisted that he only dated women who ate heartily because they inevitably had a large appetite for other sensual pleasures.

The Ford LTD with the number plate CR1 swung into the driveway of a Hutt Valley electronics firm specialising in making obscure components for the international aerospace industry. Ben sighed, pushing aside thoughts of the two great loves of his life: women and food.

He had managed to give the PM's visit to the box-like factory a little added media interest by discovering at least one of the gizmos it manufactured was being used by NASA in the new replacement for the Space Shuttle. There were two newspaper cameras and a television news crew waiting outside the factory's glassed foyer.

"Good. It must be a slow news day. We might even get a slot in the evening news with this," he said, leaning forward over the front seat towards his boss.

Murdoch grunted as he wrenched the door handle open. He liked to sit in the front of the LTD, especially when there were cameras around. It gave onlookers the impression he was an ordinary Kiwi bloke. Only ponces rode in the back of limos.

Ponces and spin-doctors, Ben grimaced to himself as Murdoch launched himself out of the still moving vehicle. One day he would nose dive into the pavement doing that. Leaping out of the car as it ground to a halt on the scoria gave the Prime Minister a very 'active', vigorous look for the cameras. Nothing looked worse on the news than the car grinding to a halt and someone slowly levering their bulk out of the seat and lumbering over to a welcoming party. By contrast, Murdoch's jet-propelled entry rocketed him across the footpath, through two handshakes and into the building in the blink of an eye.

"Thank Christ they had the glass door open for him," McGrath said over Ben's shoulder.

"Danny, what on earth brings you out here this morning?" His early warning system was wailing. It was only 9 am and McGrath had dragged himself out of bed, out of the press gallery, out to the Hutt Valley. He was not here to look at NASA gadgets.

"I like the air out here. It's nice to get out of Parliament every now and again and witness the economic miracle at work in the country's industrial heartland."

"Danny," Ben admonished, "you don't give a rat's arse about this place. What are you after?"

"What do they make here?" said McGrath, looking around puzzled.

"Gizmos for spacecraft."

"I always wondered what they looked like. I've had a long held interest in the space programme." McGrath wandered inside past the line of welcoming executives, hands clasped behind his back, in a reasonable facsimile of a member of the Royal Family on walkabout. Ben groaned inwardly and followed.

"Since when have you been interested in space?"

"Since I saw that movie with Tom Hanks. Great story. Apollo 13. I wonder if these guys made any parts for that one?"

"Oh great. Why don't you go and ask them. Say, you guys make anything that blows up spaceships? That'll go down well, Dan. At least it might get rid of you. They'd have you out of here in ten seconds flat."

"Did you hear the story about Neil Armstrong, Ben? I saw it on the wires the other day. We all know the speech he made when the *Eagle* landed on the moon, 'One small step for Man, one giant leap for Mankind,' but what did he say when he left the moon?"

Ben shook his head. McGrath was in one of his maddeningly obscure moods and it was better to humour him until it was clear what he was plotting.

"He said, Bradshaw old boy, as he climbed back into the landing module . . . he said, 'Good luck, Mr Gorsky.'"

Despite himself Ben was intrigued. "Good luck, Mr Gorsky?"

Danny McGrath nodded. "For years people have wondered what he meant by that cryptic phrase. Was it some kind of secret code to NASA, telling them he had seen signs of extra-terrestial life? Was it something to do with the Russians? You know Americans and their love of conspiracy theories. For years people debated all the theories in the papers and on things like the Internet."

McGrath paused a few paces away from the Prime Minister, who was being shown a machine that looked like a giant electric blender.

"Finally, last month, Neil Armstrong was giving one of his rare speeches to some space-type conference in Miami. During questions afterwards someone stood up and asked what he had meant by 'Good luck, Mr Gorsky.'"

Ben shook his head, "Go on."

"Well. Armstrong shuffled about a bit embarrassed and

then confessed. When he was a kid growing up he lived next door to the Gorsky family. One day, when he was about ten years old, he kicked a ball over the fence and went over to get it. While he was by their bedroom window he heard Mrs Gorsky yelling at Mr Gorsky, 'Oral sex? You want oral sex? You'll get oral sex when that skinny kid next door walks on the moon!'"

The resulting involuntary snort of laughter from Ben turned several heads as the Prime Minister was escorted into a back room where small pieces of electronic circuitry were grafted onto slightly larger pieces of circuitry. Murdoch peered knowledgeably at the scrambled wires.

"You made that up, Danny."

"It's gospel."

"Crap. What's the purpose of that little story?" Ben placed a hand on McGrath's chest, propelling him back from the group around them, who were craning their necks to watch Murdoch put on a white coat and plastic helmet. "Oh, Christ. Not the silly hats," groaned Ben. "How many times have I told him, don't wear the silly hats."

"Bradshaw, old boy," Danny McGrath interrupted. "It may be a wild conspiracy theory. There may be nothing to it. However, I need to talk to your man Murdoch about the Energy Corporation share float before it takes place tomorrow."

The internal early warning system was flashing Condition Red. The Government had been covertly moving to privatise the monolithic state-owned Energy Corporation for several months. The media might suspect the float was imminent but McGrath could not possibly know the deal was due to be signed within twenty-four hours.

"What about Energycorp?"

McGrath looked over his shoulder and saw the TV crew was well out of earshot, filming the helmeted Prime Minister sitting in what appeared to be a large ejector seat. Murdoch was grinning broadly from beneath the brim of the hat, waving at the cameras. "Great. On the front page of tomorrow's *Dominion* he'll look like Forrest Gump in orbit," muttered Ben distractedly.

"Don't try and change the subject, Bradshaw old chum." McGrath shot Ben a calculating look. "This is not like the great asset sales of the past, like Post or Forestry. Here we have a merchant bank working both sides of the deal. The bank's both selling the thing on behalf of the Government and brokering the deal for the US buyer. We also have a chief executive copping big bucks from the Yanks to keep his mouth closed and do nothing to threaten the sale. Plus, the Minister who approved the hiring of the merchant bank . . . that Minister has a wife. That wife has just bought a large share holding in both the American company that is the purchaser of Energycorp and the aforesaid merchant bank. Two companies, I may say, that will experience a huge share price increase tomorrow morning when the news comes out. I'd like to put a few questions about all that to the PM, mate."

Ben rolled his eyes and affected a shrug. He delivered his obligatory 'there is nothing new in this, it's all above board' speech and promised to see if Murdoch could spare a few minutes to put his mind at rest over the issue.

Leaving McGrath chatting to a young woman in a white lab coat about the merits of the space shuttle, Ben sauntered around the corner of the display to where the PM was having tea and biscuits, still with the hard hat perched on his head.

Politicians either have cast-iron bladders or develop

serious kidney problems later in life, Ben decided. Every visit they made invariably involved at least one compulsory cup of tea or coffee. On the campaign trail a candidate might visit a dozen or more locations in a day, meaning the forced consumption of approximately three to four pots of tea a day. By the end of a five-week stint on the campaign trail the candidate's caffeine and tannin exposure reached Chernobyl-like levels.

Quietly Ben steered Murdoch away from the group, whispering the news of McGrath's discovery.

Murdoch cursed and suggested they simply deny everything or refuse all comment citing reasons of commercial confidentiality.

That was tempting, Ben conceded, but it would not work. He had already flirted with the idea but, depending on how solid his evidence was, McGrath would simply print the damaging allegations along with the PM's weak 'neither confrim nor deny' response. The public uproar would be enough to send the share float into a tailspin and almost certainly result in the Americans' pulling out. Worse, Murdoch then would be inextricably linked to the scandal.

"You'll have to talk with McGrath. Let's get him up to your office this afternoon just before the House sits. We'll work through a defence." Murdoch grunted his approval and returned to the group of company executives hovering nearby.

McGrath was now pursuing the young lab-coated woman. When Ben gestured for him to come over, he reluctantly tore himself away from the corner where he had her pinned.

"No doorstep interview, Danny. This is too important for a quick off-the-cuff line or two from the PM. He'll see you in his office at ten minutes to two this afternoon. That will give him time to get fully briefed."

The journalist smiled, knowing he had struck gold on this story. He brushed the wrinkled sleeves of his blue blazer and tightened the tortured knot of a sadly stained silk tie that could pass as a scratch'n'sniff menu from the Boulcott Brasserie.

"I promise I won't piss on the carpet, Ben. And I'll be gentle with him."

It was a sound move to have McGrath up to the PM's office. It was Murdoch's home turf and he would feel more confident there. McGrath would be flattered at being invited into the inner sanctum and being given the Prime Minister's undivided attention. However, the timing of the meeting meant Murdoch could put his case to McGrath and there would be only a few minutes left for any tricky questions from the reporter before he was called away to the House.

The big problem was how to construct a reasonably airtight case for Murdoch to put in rebuttal and, hopefully, scuttle the story or at least soften its impact.

Disclosure was always best. It need not be the whole truth but the best defence always consisted of at least part of the truth and nothing but the truth. The most damaging of the truths could be ignored or omitted but, even if they were subsequently discovered, they would not be as wounding as the collapse of an elaborately constructed cover-up constructed of falsehoods.

Later, this logic would prove harder to defend with Simon Small. The three of them sat around the large wooden desk a succession of great Prime Ministers had used. Murdoch felt comfortable behind the assumed shield of their collective mana.

Small was in a lecturing mood.

"Ben, you really are far too honest for the Prime Minister's good, let alone your own. The strategy is simple. We deny everything. Energycorp can get an immediate *ex parte* High Court injunction against McGrath's paper to prevent them running it, stating the allegations are unfounded and citing the immeasurable commercial damage publication would cause. The Minister can threaten libel if any reference is made to him or his wife having any pecuniary interest in the share float. The merchant bankers can join the action."

"The problem is, Simon, we know McGrath is right." Ben was wasting his time with someone like Small, to whom the entire concept of truth was an anathema, but he felt he may as well give it a try.

"Who the hell cares about truth!" Small bellowed. "This will wreck us if it gets out. Let's tie the damn paper up in the courts till well after the campaign. Christ, the Energy people can tie the press up in legal action for the next two years if necessary and injunct anyone else who makes a move to publish the same stuff."

"Or, Simon," drawled Ben, "we could try the unusual ploy of being honest. We could express our shock at the revelations, institute a Commission of Inquiry into the affair, sack the Minister and put the sale on hold till a fair tender process can be established. If we lie, Simon, this is going to come back and bite us on the arse."

"Don't be silly, Ben," growled Murdoch, effectively putting an end to further argument.

Simon Small grinned with satisfaction. "Here's how I see it, Prime Minister. I'll let the Energy folk know they need to hightail it down to the High Court for that injunction. That will immediately gag the paper. Hell, the editor won't even know what hit him, he won't even be in the judge's chambers when it's granted. The first the paper will know is when it's hit with the restraint. In the meantime, sir," he went on with a rush, "you should talk to McGrath. Tell him we're satisfied that the merchant bank maintained Chinese walls throughout this transaction. That the buying wing of the bank never had any contact with the selling wing. Secondly, you have mounted your own independent internal inquiry and established that it is not unusual that a chief executive of an SOE would receive a bonus payment in the event of a successful share float and sale of the corporation." Small was on a roll. "Thirdly, the internal inquiry has disclosed no evidence that the Minister had any pecuniary involvement, he has bought no shares and received no personal benefit from the sale."

"Simon," Ben said, "the issue was not that the Minister got a kickback but that his wife used inside knowledge to buy shares and thereby gain from the deal."

"Lord! Bradshaw! I thought you were a professional? You don't answer a question like that. You only need to appear to answer it. The Prime Minister couldn't possibly comment on the financial affairs of a ministerial spouse. Surely these women have a right to live their own lives and invest how they will."

"McGrath won't buy this crap, Simon."

"He doesn't have to, Ben. We have him gagged by the injunction. The PM's line to McGrath is simply to get a cover story circulating through the gossip mill."

Ben sighed and explained to the Prime Minister he was free to follow Small's bad advice but they were simply creating a ticking time bomb that would explode at some future date.

"Maybe, but at least it won't explode now or during the election campaign," was Murdoch's verdict. "However," he went on, "that little bugger will have to go."

"Precisely which little bugger, Prime Minister?" asked Ben in his most patient voice.

He was referring to the Honourable David Barlow, the Minister with the entrepreneurial wife. Murdoch had always distrusted him for being too smart and this latest revelation was confirmation of the fact.

"I'll sack him. Get him up here before I see McGrath. Barlow's head on platter might placate him a little. I'll say he needed a well-deserved rest, pressure of work, chance to explore new avenues in a post MMP environment. You know the sort of crap, Ben."

"Also, find out who leaked this to McGrath," demanded Small. "We have to shut them up."

Ben knew already. He had made a few inquiries around the office. Wellington was an incestuously small city and very little happened without it being witnessed by someone.

In this case Julie the press secretary mentioned she had seen McGrath at an Energy Corporation cocktail party just two days ago and he had been bailed up by the SOE's public relations chief, the fearsome Zoe Harris. She later saw Zoe and McGrath heading along Courtenay Place towards the Opera Bar.

"Bingo!" yelled Small. "The bitch spilled her guts to him."

"What you going to do, Simon, fire her?" asked Ben, although he suspected he knew what was coming next.

"Fire her? Hell no. I feel like hiring the devious cow to work here. She's simply pissed off she didn't get a cut of the action like her chief executive did and this is her way of screwing some hush money out of the Americans. It'll work too. Her bonus cheque and a confidentiality agreement will be in the mail, once I tell the Yanks she was the leak."

"Dear God," groaned Ben theatrically as he wandered back to his own office. "That's it. They're all mad. There's no hope."

He threw his arms up as he walked past Julie's desk. "The world's gone crazy. Disloyalty is rewarded. Honesty will land you up in court."

"Yes, Ben," smiled the the young blonde, who barely paused at her word processor. Julie was used to her boss launching into comic outbursts of mock despair.

Except this time Ben stared down on Bowen Street and did not feel at all humorous. I feel, he thought, like I need a shower. Worse, he realised, Danny McGrath would be convinced the writ and the cover-up were his work.

"Bugger you, Small. Bugger you." He kicked the rubbish bin and brooded.

As it turned out, however, not everything went according to the Government's plan. While the Court dutifully granted the injunction and McGrath's story was stillborn, the time bomb began ticking.

Benjamin Bradshaw's favourite dictum was, 'Hell hath no fury like a hack scorned.' And so it proved.

Furious, near meltdown, Danny McGrath ascended to the Bellamy's third-floor bar known as 3.2. The curious nickname came from the sign above its entrance designating its floor and corridor number. In 3.2 McGrath proceeded to get wildly drunk and blurt his entire suppressed scoop to anyone who would listen, including Chris Cross.

At the same time, six floors above, a surprised Don Murdoch was being told a very definitive "No!" by the Honourable David Barlow. He would not resign. Murdoch could try and sack him if he liked but he would quit the Government and form his own party. Could Murdoch stand the bad press that would be generated and the increased scope for scandal during the election campaign?

The answer for Murdoch was also no.

A cocky Barlow left the Prime Minister to fume.

"I should do what my predecessor did. As soon as he appointed a Minister he got them to sign an undated resignation letter and kept it in his bottom drawer. Something went wrong, he whipped it out, called a press conference and you were out on your ear before you knew it."

Murdoch stomped off towards his private suite through the back door of his office. "What does it mean, Ben? When I can't even fire one of my own Ministers? You want a drink?"

"No, Prime Minister. I won't. I have to go down and check out 3.2. The girls tell me McGrath is on the warpath down there, babbling how we've gagged him."

Murdoch's head shot back through the door. "Is that a problem?"

"Damn right it's a problem," said Ben. "I'll go down and check it out. If it's getting too ugly I'll get you to come on down later and you can put your version of the story to the hacks over a few drinks. A little inside bully might help keep a lid on this."

However, when he walked into the bar it was obvious it was going to be difficult to find a lid large enough.

A crowd of a dozen journalists howled catcalls and cheerful abuse as he came through the doors. Propped against the bar McGrath grinned malevolently and, beside him, Christopher Cross raised a glass in mock salute.

In the corner on a sofa Julie rolled her eyes upward and aimed a gun-like finger at her temple while beside her, laughing, Susan drew a Chanel Vermilion fingernail delicately across her own throat.

In the nanosecond it took for the impending humiliation to register, Ben decided the best defence was to defect. He pulled a rolled-up Murdoch speech from his inside pocket and held it like a dagger to his stomach.

"Ah, so sorry," he moaned in a bad Japanese accent. "Such shame. Such humiliation. I must do the only honourable thing. Only, honourable choice is seppuku! hara-kiri!" He plunged the speech deep into his ample stomach and staggered theatrically across the carpet on his knees, gagging, clutching at McGrath's legs.

The crowd shrieked with delight and McGrath hissed, "You bastard," as Ben clawed his way up the journo's recoiling body.

"This story will come out and it will destroy the Government." McGrath was not about to let Ben escape so easily.

"Too right. Buggered if I'll vote for them," Ben said deadpan, reaching for the whisky the barman placed automatically on the bar in front of him.

There was another appreciative roar from the gathered journalists. There was little collective loyalty among the gallery hacks. They hunted as a pack and the gallery enjoyed seeing the discomfiture of any of its number who strayed off in search of a scoop. Had McGrath's story got to print, many would have been glad to run almost unchallenged any rebuttal the Prime Minister's Office chose to make.

Sensing both the crowd's mood and attention shift inflamed McGrath even more than the several lagers he had already downed. "I swear, Bradshaw, I will nail that bastard's hide to the wall. We will finish him!" Cross gently laid a hand on McGrath's sleeve but the journalist angrily pulled his arm away. "Murdoch will pay heavily for this crap. I promise you."

Ben looked down into his glass and nodded gently. The gesture seemed to calm McGrath, who snorted and turned his back as he began earnestly whispering to Cross.

Over the next half hour several gallery journalists broke from the bunch around Cross and McGrath, edging up to Ben claiming they, too, had the same story days ago but had chosen not to run it because of the obvious legal problems. They were ego-salvaging lies yet Ben put on his best credulous expression and agreed they were very wise. He told them to hang around, the PM was likely to come down and he might have something to say on the whole affair. Off the record, of course.

Eventually McGrath and Cross made a loud departure for a restaurant downtown and Ben gave Julie a subtle signal to collect Murdoch and bring him down to Bellamy's.

Susan missed little and strolled across to lean on her elbows on the bar beside Ben. "Danny was right. You have behaved like an absolute bastard, you know," she whispered.

"Ah, Susan. The whole placed is infested with bastards. It's contagious. This is a filthy trivial little business. It's time I got out and got into some lucrative PR consultancy somewhere."

It was a familiar theme for them both. Drinking, Ben would get maudlin and lament the course his life had taken since coming into the sphere of the politicians. Susan would be drawn into the gravitational pull of his depression and find herself mourning her own lost self-respect.

This time they were pulled up short by Murdoch's cheery

arrival. His easy confidence was such that an outside observer would not have picked this was a politician precariously balanced on the razor edge of a scandal. Gesturing with one stubby finger for the barman to get a round of drinks for the assembled media, Don Murdoch peered around with puzzlement.

"There's been a bit of a fuss, I hear?"

Encouraged by the titter of laughter at McGrath's expense the Prime Minister spent much of the next hour casually demolishing the story, using Simon Small's suggested cover-up as defence.

Even if Cross exposed the deal in Parliament, carefully edited renditions of the Prime Minister's invented version of events would be run, unattributed, in 'think' columns and comment pieces throughout the nation's media. While the Court injunction ensured full details of McGrath's story would never be printed, the Murdoch revisionist line on the sale of Energycorp would ultimately gain the most exposure.

"Chris will try and break this in the House. He will ask questions. He will use the general debate. There is enormous political capital to be made out of it," Susan whispered to Ben. "He won't let this one go once he gets his teeth into it."

Ben nodded.

"Then what's the point?" she asked.

"There is none, Sweetie. There is none," he said, downing his drink.

She smiled slyly. "This wasn't your work, was it, darling?"

Ben laughed and slid away. When Susan got intimate and called him "darling" it was time to move on. When it came to getting a story she could be like a black widow spider. The last thing he needed was a story running on radio that seemed to distance him from the Government's Energycorp defence strategy. Murdoch would smell treachery and suspect he was a leak.

He gathered up the Prime Minister and as the lift doors slid closed Murdoch leaned against the carpeted wall saying, "I think that went rather well."

6
The Spin

It continued to go well for another three days, despite Christopher Cross's attempts to pin the Government down on the issue at question time.

In the stylised ritual of parliamentary practice an MP could ask a carefully honed question and even a follow-up inquiry but there was no obligation for the Government to say anything that even remotely resembled a reply. Ministers were well versed at evasion techniques. In this instance they simply attacked Cross for his persistence and kept restating the fact that the matter was before the courts. Other elements of Cross's attack could be deflected citing commercial confidentiality.

Simon Small directed the strategy, attempting to turn the argument into one centred on Christopher Cross's subversion of the legal process. Ben could have told him it was doomed to failure. While the media were mildly interested in Cross's allegations of wrong doing, they were utterly uninterested in some academic argument over matters of law.

While Cross chipped away at the scandal fruitlessly in Parliament, the sale of the Energy Corporation to the Americans was quickly concluded and the remaining forty-nine percent of the giant company floated with great success on the sharemarket. Ben dutifully steered the media towards recognising the massive cash windfall for the Government coffers and speculation grew about generous tax cuts and increased social services spending in the next budget.

"Dangle a carrot, Benny," Murdoch always said. "When confronted by an election, dangle that carrot. By the time they realise the carrot is smaller than they thought the election has been and gone."

Cross's attacks on the sale were relegated to the inside political pages of the nation's dailies and the television networks ignored them entirely. Only the business papers sniffed around the details of the nastier allegations and they, too, were speedily injuncted on the orders of Simon Small.

At the Prime Minister's morning briefing Ben reflected that a political aide's stocks rose and fell even faster than those of the sharemarket. Buoyed by his apparent success in repelling McGrath's Energycorp assault, Small had commanded the briefings for the past few days. Ben's contributions were limited and generally ignored by Murdoch.

"Nuked the swine," Simon boasted as he laid down the transcripts of the morning radio programmes. "Except for that bitch Lewis. She did a question and answer session on breakfast radio this morning and her boyfriend had obviously fed her a lot of inside gossip on the deal. I'd injunct the bloody radio network but Clarry Evans would have a fit."

Murdoch laughed and said, "Well, ring bloody Clarry and get him to sort it out. We appointed him to run the damn place. We can't have Susan Lewis peddling that kind of actionable trash on our own radio network, for God's sake."

"You can't do that and Clarry won't agree, either," Ben put in.

The others ignored him.

"Good idea, PM." Simon flicked a glance towards Ben. "In fact, she is hopelessly compromised by this fling with Cross. She really should be withdrawn from covering politics. I'll talk to Clarry about it."

Ben raised one eyebrow and asked, "What grounds, exactly, does Clarry have to fire her?"

"I know she's a friend of yours Ben, and it's admirable you should come to her defence," Simon postively purred, "but she is not being fired. She is being redeployed."

"What grounds would Clarry have for redeploying her then, Simon?"

"She's having an affair with Christopher Cross," said Simon with some exasperation. "Where's her journalistic objectivity?"

Ben shrugged and seemed to agree. "Yeah. Fair enough, Simon. Except we're getting onto dangerous ground here when it comes to ruling out journos who are bonking or have been bonked by politicians."

He ticked off three more gallery journalists who were pursuing liaisons with members of parliament, plus a couple more members of the Government who were attempting to pursue journos.

Murdoch was showing intense interest. "Really, I had no idea. Do we know for sure?"

"Prime Minister," said Ben, "there is no way to have proof positive that any of them are at it. Short of having Polaroids and tape recordings. By the way, Simon, I presume you have that kind of proof about Susan Lewis and Cross. If you expect Clarry to dump her he will have to have some kind of hard evidence. It will leak out and the rest of the chooks will swoop and demand to know why she's getting the chop. Clarry will need evidence. Gossip and tittle tattle from the bar will not be enough."

Small squirmed a little and admitted there was no hard proof. He shelved the idea of trying to get Susan axed but he would still try to get Evans to pressure the radio network's executives to tone down their coverage of the Energycorp scandal even if he could not sideline Lewis.

Ben knew Clarry well enough to realise that the radio network's chairman would readily agree to anything Small suggested to him and then quietly ignore the matter. Clarry Evans didn't get where he was today by being so blatant as to lay himself open to charges of naked political intereference. Anyway, Ben's old Avalon experience of the spineless broadcasting executives in television suggested that their cousins in radio would probably be able to anticipate a cold front coming in from the Beehive and pull back on their coverage without any further prompting. Whatever flak flew in the corridors of the network, Susan's position was safe. Before Ben could feel even a small level of triumph at that minor victory, Small returned to the attack.

"Daniel McGrath is another matter, however. I understand he made provocative and politically partisan remarks against the Government in the bar the other night."

The public would never understand how petty and childishly vindictive politics could become, Ben thought. Most people imagined Ministers and officials sat around in the Beehive fretting over the state of the economy or other weighty matters of state. They were wrong. Their elected representatives were obsessed with trivia.

Once, while waiting outside the wooden partition that screened the Cabinet room from the officials who gathered outside, Ben heard Ministers approve a $200 million expenditure on a new national art gallery in three minutes and then debate the positioning of its toilets for half an hour. He had heard them argue over the drinking habits of journalists, the sexual proclivities of television personalities and the plots of soap operas.

"Ben, did McGrath not call the Prime Minister a

'bastard' and claim he was 'going to pin his hide to the wall'? Did he not threaten to 'destroy the Government'?" Small was in full inquisitorial swing. "That is a flagrant breach of neutrality and objectivity."

Murdoch seemed genuinely annoyed and hurt to hear of the attack. The fact he had shamelessly lied to McGrath and potentially damaged the reporter's career seemed to escape him.

"Danny was pissed, Simon," groaned Ben. "You can't take seriously anything anyone says in 3.2."

"His editors might," said Small archly. "Prime Minister, I think you should have McGrath up to your office again. Only this time you carpet the little bugger. Tell him he either pulls his head in or you'll ring his editor and inform him of the remarks made in the bar."

Small had long advocated ruling the media by fear. He did not have a subtle bone in his scrawny body, thought Ben. Attacks on the press only alienated it further: such a move might silence Daniel McGrath in the short term or even get him fired, but it would also make him a martyr to the rest of the journalists, who would fear similar treatment. Their coverage of the Government would instantly sour as they struck back in self-defence.

It was impossible, however, to make either Small or Cross see reason and just after lunch Ben looked up from his desk to see McGrath standing by the door.

"You are a true bastard, Ben. I never thought you were capable of this. You didn't even have the guts to be there. I'm stuffed. They have me by the balls. I'll have to quit. There's no way out of this one."

"If you can't see Simon Small's fingerprints on this, Danny, you're sillier than I thought." Ben bit his lip and suddenly stood up holding a sheet of paper from his desk. "Oops. It slipped out of my hand onto the floor. I wonder where it went. Damn, I can't find it."

McGrath looked down at the photocopy on the floor in front of him. He slowly bent down and retrieved it. His eyes widened as he read it and then narrowed in suspicion as he looked back at Ben.

"Bradshaw, you are a cunning, devious prick. Why would you give me this? You know I can't print it."

"True." Ben pulled a face. "But your editor can at least see it and know you're not lying to him about the Energycorp deal. Then again, it could always fall out of your hand and some even more cunning and devious opposition politician could find it and use it under parliamentary privilege. Even those news organisations who were injuncted on the Energycorp issue would be entitled to run a news report quoting an MP speaking in Parliament."

McGrath muttered a small prayer of thanks and bounced out of the office. Seconds later he returned.

"You are an even more cunning and devious prick than I thought. The cover-up wasn't your idea. It was Small's wasn't it? This will nail that little pig. He will end up covered in crap and you will smell like roses. You will be able to say, 'See I told you so, Prime Minister.'"

Ben held his hand out for the paper. "If you feel you're being used you can give it back, Daniel."

McGrath snatched it out of Ben's reach, stuffing it in the pocket of his rumpled jacket as he fled.

The next morning's briefing session was not as pleasant as those earlier in the week. All the papers carried front page stories reporting Cross's speech in the general debate. The *Dominion* carried the headline, 'Energycorp Kickback

Scam'. The *New Zealand Herald* was more circumspect: 'Government Under Fire Over Energy Sale'. Ben's favourite was the usually staid Christchurch *Press*, which had splashed the banner headline, 'Corruption Scandal Rocks Murdoch'.

The Prime Minister's pallid complexion turned a deep shade of puce as he screwed up the *Press*.

"Can anyone tell me what on earth happened here?" he demanded.

White and visibly shaken, Small said nothing.

"I think we've been gazumped, Prime Minister," said Ben. " There was always the risk something like this would happen. In any deal as big as Energycorp a huge amount of paperwork circulates and there is always the chance some of it may fall into the hands of the Opposition."

Cornered, Murdoch could do a reasonable impression of a bassett hound, turning his imploring brown eyes on whoever offered the best hope of rescue. Right now Ben Bradshaw seemed to be the only lifeguard on duty and Ben quickly ran through the problems that now threatened to engulf them.

It seemed Cross had, somehow, obtained a merchant bank document that outlined its risk in the Energycorp deal. The paper quoted legal advice that the bank was exposed to charges of insider trading in several areas. It also detailed the bank's exposure with regard to large cash payments to the company's chief executive, who had been threatening to torpedo the sale, and share transactions made by a Cabinet Minister's wife.

The time bomb had exploded.

Ben smiled graciously. "On the positive side of the ledger, gentlemen, it does not give details of the shonky valuation on the corporation or give any information about the

Government's role in what appears to be a patent commercial carve-up of a state resource."

Murdoch groaned, "You mean Cross may have more papers, more files, and drip feed them out. We kick off the election campaign in ten days', time! I can't fight an election with this happening!"

The Prime Minister had raised the white flag. Simon Small had sunk his face into his hands and Ben had the floor to himself.

He outlined a simple mopping-up operation. Murdoch would immediately call a Commission of Inquiry into the scandal. The Prime Minister could publicly relieve the Energy Minister of his duties pending the outcome of that formal inquiry. With everything in the open, Energy Minister Barlow's threats to defect were meaningless. He would be a pariah. His best hope of political survival would be with the Government, albeit as a disgraced backbencher.

All parliamentary debate would have to cease when the House rose at the end of the week in preparation for the election campaign. Murdoch could challenge Cross to present his evidence to the inquiry and keep the details of the issue out of the campaign to prevent it influencing the outcome of the commission. It would not would entirely defuse the scandal but it would give Murdoch a good stonewall defence in press conferences and public debates.

"From what I can see, Prime Minister, at the moment the only ones carrying the can are Barlow, his beloved spouse, a couple of merchant bankers and one greedy SOE boss. I'm sure we all mourn for them but no one can lay a glove on us. Some of the muck will stick during the campaign, Cross and the damn Socialists will make a meal of it, but it is far from a complete disaster."

Murdoch's relief was palpable. For one awful second Ben thought the old man might hurdle the huge desk and hug him, but he stalled the Prime Minister by saying, "Anyway, I'd be more worried by that story on the feature page of the *Dom*."

Small roused himself and ripped open the paper. After a few seconds he found it. "The hospital hepatitis outbreak?"

"Check the source of the outbreak, Simon. Medical experts say it comes from infected surgical equipment purchased from a supplier in India. It looks like some entrepreneurial Indian orderly was collecting used butterfly clips, instruments and intravenous drip equipment, giving them a quick wash and repackaging them for shipment here."

Murdoch was frantically leafing through his own copy of the paper.

Ben went on, "As yet it's only the hospital getting the flak. However, I don't think it will take the hacks long to trace the trail back to the Health Department and from there to the Minister and Cabinet."

Ben paused at the door as he left. "Still, that's next week's scandal. We can rise to meet that challenge when it happens."

He closed the door softly.

7
The Spin

The atmosphere in the Tutaekuri Community Hall had not improved.

Murdoch pushed the power button of the fourteen-inch television on the bench and fumbled with the remote control. Like men of his vintage the power switch was all he could manage. The remote was a device best left to the care and control of his children.

Ben walked around the table and held his hand out.

"What are they saying on the other side? The other channel?" Murdoch demanded, handing it over.

"The same thing, boss. The same thing."

The mute remained on as he flicked between the two election-night broadcasts. On one a cadaverous woman stood in a brightly lit hall in front of a white wooden door, her mouth working furiously as she gestured behind her.

Ben realised with a start the reporter was three metres away on the other side of the kitchen wall. He clicked over to see a shot of Socialist leader Paul Knox at his Auckland headquarters.

"There's your other option, boss. A pact with the Devil. All you have to do is sell your soul. You could be the first Tory-Left coalition in the history of politics."

Murdoch snorted. "It doesn't have to be a coalition, Ben. He just has to give us the votes in Parliament when we need them. I know he's ruled it out but I wonder if we could reach an accommodation?"

Ben knew the strategy. All Paul Knox and the Socialists would have to do was guarantee to support the Government on confidence motions or money bills and Murdoch could survive. The price of that support, however, would be a total reversal of almost everything his Government had done in the past few years.

"An accommodation with the Socialists, PM? Over Jane Street's dead body."

"I'm sure that could be arranged, Benny."

They both laughed and flicked the television off, realising just how impossible almost any deal had become.

The kitchen filled with the racket from outside, the death rattle of the party faithful, as Simon Small launched himself back into the room.

"I'm glad you two find it funny. The whole bloody evening is absolutely hilarious." He held out his phone. "Perhaps you could explain the joke to Sir Leonard Holt. He wants to talk to you."

Holt controlled one of the country's leading trading banks. A solid contributor to the party's coffers, he was also an ardent exponent of hard-line New Right policies. Paranoid talkback radio, some elements of the press and populist politicians like Cross and Knox portrayed Holt as the machiavellian general leading the battalions of big business in a conspiracy to loot the nation of its wealth.

Murdoch stared at the cellular phone with the same bewilderment he had reserved for the television's remote control. He took it with two hands, placed it to his ear and, gaining confidence, bellowed, "Hello!" Murdoch seemed to think a phone without a cord required twice the lung power.

"Hello! Len! Are you there?"

Len was. Indeed, Sir Leonard appeared to operate on the same decibel level and he could be heard shouting back.

As the two men continued barking at each other Ben scrutinised Simon's face. For someone contemplating defeat Small seemed too content. There was a hint of a sneer at one corner of his thin lips.

Murdoch finished the call, his large fingers stabbing

repeatedly at the keypad till Simon took the phone back and snapped it shut.

The Prime Minister straightened and ran a hand through his white hair. Somewhat unnecessarily, considering the volume at which the discussion had occurred, he told the pair of Sir Leonard's warning. The run on the dollar had begun in earnest.

Three days earlier the Reserve Bank Governor had warned that the trickle of funds out of the country had turned into a steady stream. Now, according to the money dealers on the floor of Sir Leonard's trading bank, the stream had turned into a flood. The economy could not long sustain the damage inflicted by such a crisis of confidence and Holt was insisting on a speedy deal with someone like Foot or even Cross to inject some stability back into a collapsing market.

"You have no choice now, Prime Minister." A tiny trace of triumph could be heard in Simon Small's voice.

"It'll have to be Foot and the Liberals," Murdoch said quietly. "But there's still that damn Health debacle. I'll be handing him a loaded gun."

"We'll handle it . . ." Simon began.

Ben cut across him. "Let's think this through."

"What Health debacle, Don? I want to know." Faith had been an almost invisible presence in the kitchen headquarters until now. Suddenly, she slipped between Murdoch and his two advisors, insistently locking her eyes onto his. "Tell me, Don."

Simon placed a long pale hand on her shoulder. "Mrs Murdoch, I don't think now is quite . . ."

"Be quiet, Simon. I'm talking to my husband."

Small's head snapped back as though he had been

slapped, his hand hovering in the air for a moment before he hid it back in his pocket. Ben moved back a step and froze as he got a small premonition of what was to come.

Murdoch's confusion was genuine. He explained there was nothing to worry about. "Cabinet cost cutting leads to some hard decisions, Faith, and we had to make some. We needed to trim some money out of Health and the easiest way was to get the people who buy the supplies for our Health system to use the most cost-efficient suppliers."

He flicked a glance at Ben, who nodded imperceptibly.

"Faith, we had no idea of what would happen. Some of these foreign suppliers were very crooked. Much, much later we found they'd been selling us drugs from Third World plants that were terribly inferior. End of line stuff, under strength, often not really drugs at all, just rubbish. Worse, some infected surgical supplies slipped through."

Murdoch patiently explained there had been little that could be done. Once the problems had been discovered the suppliers had been dropped and different, more expensive, safer sources found. Sadly, there was little to be done about the patients who had been infected or, in some cases, killed by the mistakes. It was not the Government's fault but it would get the blame should the full story ever emerge.

Faith listened closely and when he had finished she remained quiet, thinking. Murdoch looked back at the men opposite and seemed about to begin issuing orders when Faith suddenly posed another question.

"Was there no one who checked these things? Surely there's some Government Department that checks the strength of drugs or the hygiene of surgical supplies?"

Murdoch looked momentarily annoyed, as if he thought he had laid the matter to rest, but he answered her. "Frankly no, Faith, there isn't. Do you realise how much that would cost? We rely on international standards, groups like the American Food and Drug Administration and the quality guidelines laid down by the pharmaceutical companies and medical supply outfits. Now, dear, can you give us a few moments to sort this other business out?"

Faith watched him move towards the men who worked for him, seeking shelter in the herd. She cut him off.

"It was you. You almost killed me, Don," Faith said softly. "You know that?"

It was Murdoch's turn to look as if he had been slapped. His jaw worked slackly but no sound came out.

"I mean it, Donald. Your damn Government and its damn cost cutting almost killed me."

She was a wan figure, grey and almost translucent. As a Prime Minister's wife she had attracted the least publicity of any in the last couple of decades. The invisible First Lady, a misty presence in the back of grainy newspaper shots of Murdoch attending rallies or boarding a plane in some strange foreign land. She had been even paler and less noticeable since her illness last summer.

"You remember the hysterectomy, Don? I know you don't like talking about it but we are going to. How did I overhear you describe it to Ben? Women's problems, I think you called it."

Ben flinched, guilty by association.

"Let me tell you, Donald, that operation was no problem. No problem at all, compared to what followed."

Murdoch winced as his wife strode around the table.

"I have hepatitis E. Ever heard of E?"

She glared at the three men. Shocked by the intensity of her attack all shook their heads involuntarily.

"Neither had most of the doctors. They couldn't understand it. I was recovering well and then, suddenly, I'm at death's door. You wouldn't have known, Don. You were off somewhere overseas. I think I got a phone call from you but, of course, we didn't want to worry you."

Faith took a deep breath. "Meanwhile, they did blood test after blood test and, finally, someone says it's Hepatitis E. You generally only get that in the Indian sub-continent, they told me."

Until now, Faith thought she might have unwittingly picked up the disease when she had followed her husband to a Commonwealth Heads of Government Meeting in New Delhi several years before. She thought it must have long lain dormant. Now, she realised, the disease had found her much closer to home.

"God, Donald. You insisted I had to go on a waiting list until I could get into a public hospital. You were the one who said it would look bad to go private and worse if I appeared to jump the queue. I wait, I run the risk of the cancer taking hold in me, I wait and go to your damn public hospital and . . ." Her voice had run cold as ice. "You tried to kill me with your meanness. You and your precious damn Government. Think about it, Donald. You were too bloody cheap to make sure your own wife was safe."

Murdoch was almost in a state of shock, as was Ben, who had never heard Faith swear, never seen her so vehement about anything. He had never taken any real notice of her before nor, perhaps, for many years had her husband. Murdoch looked sick, as he stared almost paralysed at her.

"I think I'll just check how things are going out in the hall," Ben said, plucking at Simon's sleeve.

"Uh. I'll help."

They scuttled out leaving the couple together and, sliding the door closed, Ben noticed Murdoch reach out to her.

Simon was again swamped by the media pack and Ben slipped along the wall behind the protective shield of a line of DPS officers. He thought he had escaped when a hand came from behind, snuck up under his jacket, reached inside his pants and hauled on the back of his underwear.

"Crutchcutter! Gotcha, Benny."

"Dear God. Brenda!"

The Prime Minister's niece released her death grip on the elastic of his boxer shorts. "How's Uncle Don getting on? The old duffer's really got to get a move on, Benny. The drinks are running out. Half the hall's gone home in a mood of black depression and that loathsome skunk McGrath is trying to fuck me. Again."

She was drunk, a fact Ben could not help but mention. Brenda simply smiled and winked.

"Oh God, save me, Benny," she suddenly wailed as Daniel McGrath slipped around the flank of the phalanx of plainclothes policemen.

"What's going on, Bradshaw? Is the man paralysed or what? Why the hell doesn't Murdoch do something?" McGrath demanded.

The sour alcoholic fallout of the hack's breath drove Ben back a step. Summoning up his courage he leaned forward and whispered in McGrath's ear, "Hold on for just half an hour, Danny, and you'll have the lot. Show some patience, man. Besides, wee Brenda here tells me she's desperate to bonk you."

McGrath cocked his head like an irish setter getting a trace of a new scent. Ben crept off and Daniel grabbed the startled woman's hand, smothering it with wet-lipped kisses.

Across the car park at the back of the hall, beside the large television outside-broadcast trucks, sat a long white caravan. It looked like part of the the television entourage. Protruding from the trailer was a thick heavy-duty power cable and several other long wires that did not look out of place alongside the outside-broadcast vans' spaghetti trail of camera and sound cables. Ben paused by the caravan door. He casually glanced around before he knocked.

As he entered he was buffeted by a babble of sound coming from a bank of radio scanners on the main table. Several tape recorders were lined up along the bench seat behind it.

"OK, boys. What have we got?" Ben asked, peering at the two men who were hunched over the radio apparatus.

"It was a good move to bring a portable setup in here, Ben," said one of the men, taking off his headphones. "We can isolate the individual cell repeaters in this district and bring in the signals very clearly. Of course, Larry's operation in Auckland and down country will be getting much more but I'm pretty confident we've got this end covered."

The tall man nodded at his companion, "We're not the GCSB but when it comes to this level of sigint we can match anything they pull in."

He was talking of the Government's electronic eavesdropping unit, the Government Communications Security Bureau, which monitored phone, fax and computer traffic around the country and throughout the Pacific providing signals intelligence or sigint.

"Just tell me what you're getting," Ben said. Both free-lancers were former GCSB spooks with long backgrounds in the military and would happily blather on for hours using acronyms, delighting in their own cleverness.

"Well, the media are in a lather. You tell your boss they're all about to launch into stories of constitutional crisis if he doesn't come out and face them in the next few minutes."

"Forget the media," Ben interrupted. "What do you hear on the financial front?"

"Well, a lot of that particular sigint is being relayed from Larry's monitoring set-ups in Auckland and Wellington. They're picking up frantic cellphone traffic from the money market boys, who are all scurrying into work from home for a bit of late-night trading. "

"Go on."

The tall man shrugged. "Larry says it's weird. He's picking up panic calls from all the major banks and institutions except one. Strangely enough, the certain bank you warned us to watch out for hasn't been heard from. Not a murmur on the phone from anyone who works for them."

His companion nodded and chipped in, "Although everyone else in the money business is talking about your particular friends at the bank. A lot of the calls that Larry's intercepted are asking what the hell your man Sir Leonard Holt thinks he's doing."

He searched around a pile of cassettes stacked on the table and slammed one in a cassette player. "Listen to this, Ben. We picked this one up ourselves."

The machine rolled and a crackling voice could be heard over a car engine.

"I'm on my way back from Turangi now. That lunatic Holt has stuffed my weekend's fishing. I hope he dies a horrible death in hell."

Another voice replied, "That crazy bastard's going to

ruin us all. We can't let him sell down the Kiwi for too much longer. There's a very real danger we could get stranded if we don't start to match him. The question is, how long we can hold out?"

The frustrated fisherman cut in, "Shit, I'd love to stick to our position on the Kiwi, have the market bounce back and watch the beloved Sir Len bleed through the ears as he was forced to suck air on his losses."

"That's the danger, Bernie, that's the danger in leading the market and playing the games that he plays. It could turn around and bite him on the arse. What do you reckon we should do?"

"I'll be there in four hours. We hold till then. I might even make it in three and half hours if the roads stay clear and they should at this time of night. We'll reassess our position as soon as I'm back. Hopefully that moron Murdoch might have made up his own mind by then."

The spook switched off the machine and looked inquiringly at Ben, who stood staring at the tape recorder, nodding to himself.

"Right, boys. What else?"

They shuffled nervously. The tall spook looked wordlessly at his companion before picking up another cassette and playing it. He glanced speculatively at Ben before he turned away and faced the wall.

Jane Street's strident voice came over the speaker.

"He must be made to see reason, Simon. If you can't get him to do the right thing then you'll have to call me straight back. I have an undertaking from everyone who matters in caucus that if Don cannot come to an arrangement with Cross then he will have to go. The Deputy Prime Minister tells me his relations with Christopher Cross are fine, that they can work together. Of course, the weasel says as Deputy PM he can't move against Murdoch himself, I'll have to orchestrate the entire coup so he keeps his hands clean and appears loyal."

"If he's that gutless, do we want him at all?" Simon Small's voice was harsh. "Murdoch doesn't have to be replaced by his deputy. It could be you."

"Very flattering, Simon dear, but we have to look at reality. Caucus will buy Murdoch's demise if we make the change with little fuss and install our esteemed deputy in his place. He's bland, diplomatic and non-threatening. If I were to put my name forward there would be a much broader caucus battle and Murdoch might survive."

"Yes, well, you're probably right," said Simon. 'But we've got to do something quickly. We've created a monster with Holt. He's not just started a run on the dollar, it's a rout. Can you call him and tell him to ease up?"

"Certainly not. Holt is doing just fine, it's just what we all talked about. This is exactly the scenario we had planned. It forces Murdoch's hand and, indeed, neatly ensures he has nowhere to go." Jane Street added with relish, "Sorry, Don. Checkmate."

"Well, the question now is not how we roll Murdoch but when." Small was thinking hard. "There won't be another caucus meeting for weeks. If he has to go, then he has to be got rid of quickly."

"If a majority of his Cabinet went to him and said he no longer had their support, then he would have to go. If necessary, Cabinet could go to the Governor-General and inform him that the Prime Minister no longer enjoyed the confidence of his ministers. It's happened before and we can do it again."

Ben pushed 'Stop' and motioned for the tape to be rewound. He slipped it into his jacket pocket.

"Well, anything else, chaps? You didn't pick up the army mobilising for a military coup? The Russians planning a pre-emptive nuclear strike? Aliens landing in Eden Park saying, 'Take us to your leader'? Come to think of it, right now we might be hard pressed to figure out who to take the aliens to." Ben laughed but the spooks remained soberly straight faced.

The tall Spook had taken the question seriously. "Now you mention it, there is a hell of a lot of traffic coming out of the US embassy, but it's all coded and scrambled. Only the GCSB could crack it. We could try and find out if you want."

"No, guys, I think international espionage is where I draw the line. Great work, keep going, I'll be back later."

Ben was halfway out the door when the quieter spook spoke up. "Oh, we have one other great call recorded here. We taped it earlier. It sounds like Christopher Cross talking to a woman, presumably a woman in or around the headquarters here. There's, um, a lot of Cross making some rather lewd suggestions about what he'd like to be doing to her. He called her . . . let's see, I have a note of it here. Ah, yes. Her name was Susan . . ."

"That's OK, guys. I don't think I need to hear it." Ben turned away.

"Anyway, the phone sex didn't come to much. She ended up having a huge row with him."

Ben stopped and closed the door, waiting for the talkative tall spook to continue.

"Basically, it seems he told her even though he was leaving his wife after the election he still couldn't be seen to have an open relationship with her. Cross told the girl that marriage was out of the question and they would have to play it very close to the chest when he was in Government. That's when she went ballistic."

Ben thanked the men and, as he left, he told them to erase that tape.

8

The Spin

Susan had decided it was not a wise move to cover the Cross campaign and had assigned herself to following the Prime Minister for the hectic five weeks leading up to the election.

She sat in the back row of Murdoch's chartered passenger plane as it taxied slowly towards the end of the Wellington runway for takeoff. Ben and Julie were doing a ruthless rendition of the standard hostie routine. He provided the commentary, Julie did the actions.

On the words, "Have you seen this?" the gallery pack howled and catcalled as the young press secretary flashed her pants. The demonstration ended in chaos with Julie, who had bound herself with a seat belt strap, performing the role of the oxygen mask descending toward Daniel McGrath's beaming face.

To cheers and applause she scrambled shrieking out of McGrath's octopus grip and into a seat across the aisle. Ben slumped down beside Susan.

"Pathetic and childish, Benny," said Susan from behind a copy of *Cleo*.

"This from a woman reading . . ." He glanced at the page she had open. "'Fifty Ways to Please Your Lover'?"

"Nothing will please him," she said crisply.

"What about number thirty-seven?" said Ben, peering incredulously at the magazine and pulling it towards him.

She gently slapped his hand and closed the *Cleo*. "Not even in your wildest dreams, sunshine. Or his, for that matter. The louse." She sighed. "Oh, Benny, what's a dame supposed to do? Last night in Auckland Chris had that big public meeting at the Aotea Centre. He gets such a buzz out of the crowd and the adulation he's still bouncing around at one in the morning. I'm staying at the Carlton, he's got no one to play with and suddenly he's knocking on my door. In the middle of the night it's, 'Hi, honey, I'm home.' How's that for barefaced cheek."

The plane dipped sharply in the air currents above Cook Strait and Susan grasped Ben's hand.

He looked at the cabin ceiling. "Barearsed cheek actually, according to the DPS guy who was watching your floor. He tells me Chris snuck out around six o'clock, sweetie."

She flushed. "They're spying on me? Jesus, is there no privacy here?"

"They're the security detail, sweetie. They watch everything that happens in the hotels where Murdoch stays."

Susan shook her head in disgust and Ben gently reassured her the DPS would remain discreet. "They like you. I think Tony, the big guy with the moustache, is secretly in love with you himself. I'm the only one he told and the only one that will know."

She demanded a promise the information would never make the X-files in his desk drawer.

"Only the Polaroids," he laughed.

She gasped and punched him none too gently on the shoulder.

"Joke, sweetie. Joke."

The Marlborough Sounds crept underneath the plane and Susan concentrated on watching the view for few minutes.

"You think I'm a silly slut, don't you, Ben?" she said eventually. He shook his head. "You wouldn't be the only one. I'm like some second-class citizen. There is nothing worse than being a Wellington mistress. You are automatically assigned to concubine status. You know what that cow Charlotte has done to me?"

Ben raised his eyebrows. Charlotte was a long-time friend of Susan's. While Susan had pursued her doomed affair with Cross, Charlotte had cut a Cabinet Minister out from the herd, roped, tackled and branded him as her own. It had taken three years but finally the Minister had shed his sad first wife and stuck an engagement ring on Charlotte's finger.

"You got an invitation to their wedding, didn't you?" Susan demanded.

Ben nodded.

"I got an invitation to drinks," she breathed through clenched teeth. "No wedding invitation for me. No bridal shower. No invite to the hen party. The wedding is reserved for wives, power-brokers and colleagues." Tears more of frustration than sadness welled in the corners of her eyes. "Look, Benny, I don't give a shit about that stuff really – it was the knowledge that the damn hen night and bridal shower were exclusively reserved for the political wives and her other legitimately married friends. She has drinks at her flat for the pariahs who are mistresses or divorced and therefore a threat to her new-found respectability as a political wife. Jesus. The hypocrisy of that woman. She screws a married man for three years, weeps on my shoulder about it continually, and then when she finally hooks him, she cuts me dead. Bitch."

Susan folded her arms in an angry huff and kicked the seat in front of her.

"Well, Susie, you know the pressures that would have come on her," Ben explained. How could Charlotte carve a place with the Cabinet and backbench wives if she flaunted her former concubine status in front of them? How could she have Susan and the wife of, say, a Minister together in the same room? The woman would probably know of Susan's involvement with Cross and begin wondering whether her own husband was staying faithful after all those long, lonely late-night sittings in Wellington.

Also, Ben pointed out, how could Charlotte's new ministerial hubby tolerate hosting a political enemy's lover? Besides, the chances were Charlotte had to show some loyalty to her fiance's position. If hubby hated Chris then she must hate him too and so she now hated Susan by proxy.

Susan was looking at him with frozen disgust. Ben sealed his fate by continuing, "Bottom line, Susie. You're still a mistress. Charlotte the Harlot's now climbed another step up the Wellington ladder of respectability and she cannot resist reminding you of it."

Susan was concentrating her famous death stare on Ben when he was given a lucky escape by Murdoch, who had bounded back through the curtain that divided the hacks from the political staff.

A big-breasted young girl in her late teens sashayed down the aisle, behind him. Up front McGrath immediately lost all interest in attempting to entice Julie back across the aisle, and she looked a little miffed despite herself. The other journalists craned over their seats as the PM and his young companion passed. Even the earnest Press Association reporter looked up briefly from the laptop computer he had been pounding.

He introduced his niece. "You know my brother Ned's girl? Brenda's going to be travelling the campaign trail with us. She's a political science student at Auckland University, wants to be a journalist or PR person one day. This is perfect experience for her. She can help you out, Ben."

She leaned back on the arm-rest across the aisle and

smiled prettily, but Ben found it difficult to tear his eyes off the ring through her navel. Her midriff was tanned and quite taut.

"I work out," she said quietly, having followed his gaze. "You like the navel ring? Everybody said it would hurt but it didn't."

Ben's adam's apple was working overtime.

Murdoch peered down at Ben and patted his arm as he walked off. "Look after her, Ben."

"Perhaps, you can tutor her in your more than ample spare time at nights, Benny," Susan said sweetly.

"Ah. Yes. Thank you, Susan. Um, Brenda, this is Susan Lewis. She's a journalist."

The two women exchanged small, shrewd, appraising looks and Brenda asked who Susan worked for. Ben sensed the cabin temperature drop when Brenda said, "Radio? Oooh. I'd only work for television. It looks so much more fun. Don't you think, Ben?"

He struggled to get out of the seat as the sharp end of Susan's elbow dug deeply into his tender side. "Actually, I used to work for television myself, Brenda, and I can tell you it is not that glamorous."

Brenda thought for a second and then said she thought she could recall watching him when she was a little girl. Ben could hear Susan's snicker of revenge as he steered Brenda back up the aisle. "Pass me my walking frame, Brenda," he said through clenched teeth.

"What would you like me to do first, Ben?" she asked, smiling at the journalists, most of whom were still sitting mouths agape.

"Perhaps you could slip into something less comfortable," suggested Ben. Although, when he thought about it, hip-hugging black jeans and a skin-tight white halter top that ended far north of the navel and just south of her breasts might be just the thing to make hacks like McGrath a little less critical of the Murdoch campaign. He could sense the rising level of testosterone in the cabin, although the ceiling was beginning to drip venom from the women on board.

"Why don't you sit here with Danny McGrath," said Ben. McGrath mouthed a silent "Yesss!" of gratitude and Ben added, "You'll know Danny from his by-lines. Danny's had more election campaigns than you've had hot pants, uh, dinners. Let him give you some insight into the mind of the working journalist. I've just got to pop up front for a quick word with Uncle Don about tonight's big opening rally at the Christchurch town hall."

He left them deep in shallow conversation and dived through the curtain where Murdoch was working through his speech.

"Turn the page of history . . ." He was reading it to Simon Small or, more precisely, rewording it and delivering it to Small.

"No. The line reads, 'And so we prepare to turn another page in history'," explained Ben, squatting down beside Murdoch. "What you're saying is, we are about to enter a new era in which the past is left behind and we start anew."

"I like challenging people to do it themselves, you know." Murdoch insisted.

"But it doesn't make sense, Prime Minister." Ben pointed to the speech. "See, you go on to say, 'and begin a whole new chapter in the life of this country'."

"Well, Ben," Simon said, smiling patronisingly, "I appreciate every word is a gem but the PM wants to give it a little sharper edge. He now says, 'Turn the page of history and write your own with two strokes of the pen for the Government.' I think you'll concede the Prime Minister has come up with something a little better? It pushes the double tick message quite nicely."

Dear Lord, Ben prayed quietly. He had spent much of the past fortnight crafting Murdoch's opening address for the campaign. It had been honed to give him a subtle sense of statesmanship and refined to portray him as a man of genuine vision. In this latest mutilated version Murdoch would sound like he was flogging a pig in a barrow raffle in the public bar of the Tutaekuri pub.

He looked down at the pages strewn across the table, covered in ballpoint scribble. "Did you come up with the line about the 'thousand points of light', Prime Minister?"

"Ah, no. That may have been Simon's."

"Well, George Bush beat him to it and used it first," said Ben wearily. "No one understood what Bush meant by it either and, as I recall, Bill Clinton kicked his arse in that election."

The pair agreed to drop it but were determined to press ahead with the rewritten version.

Do I try honesty or lie? Ben thought. He lied.

"I'm sure it will go down well with the party faithful," he said. As only the party faithful would be let into the hall, Murdoch would be certain of a warm reception. If he stood up on the podium, had a stroke and collapsed gurgling, he would still get warm applause. This was a ticket-only affair and while a few stirrers and demonstrators might sneak in, they would be easily contained.

It was the television audience at home that mattered most. Ben and the advertising agency men had prepared a slick commercial introduction that would lead into Murdoch's rousing welcome by the troops in the hall. He had kept the speech as short as possible and scheduled another long commercial to run off the end of Murdoch's address.

They had tested this approach out on one of their pollster's focus groups. The people had been made to watch a mock-up programme, similar to the real campaign launch, which used the new commercials at the beginning and end. An edited version of an old Murdoch campaign speech from the last election was inserted in the middle to give a feeling of what it would be like on the night.

The focus group research showed people were left with three overwhelming impressions: the images of the opening commercial, the sight of Murdoch being mobbed and greeted rapturously in the hall, and the final positive images of the closing commercial. Not a single member of the group could correctly recall one fact from the speech itself. All felt more positively towards Murdoch and the Government than they had before.

They had toyed with the idea of not doing a live broadcast or including a speech by Murdoch. It had become popular to use the available television time to air documentary-style items extolling the virtues of the party. However, it had been decided that this was a presidential-type campaign and it was essential to include as much of the Prime Minister as possible. The focus group research backed up this decision. The old style leader's rally could be a winner.

Later, on the huge stage of the Christchurch town hall during rehearsals, Ben reassured himself that Murdoch could announce he favoured necrophilia as a recreational option and his approval rating would still rise, as long as the television production itself was smooth and seamless.

Sitting cross-legged in the centre aisle, Brenda waved to him and he found himself walking down to see her. She had certainly managed to keep McGrath and some of the other boys on the campaign bus on side. The hacks had a nasty habit of whining when they were gathered together for too long and, after a while, that negative attitude began to filter through in their copy about the candidate. If Brenda kept their mood up and their attention focused away from any potential screw-ups, then she was earning her keep.

"Cool show, Ben. It'll look fine." She smiled her approval from behind a pair of Ray Bans.

"Thanks."

"'Cept that warm-up guy really sucks. Who's he supposed to be?" she asked.

Ben shrugged. He had missed the warm-up act. It was designed to get the crowd in the mood for cheering and clapping. Usually a local comedian was hired for the occasion. Often the party had used high-profile pop singers to get the crowd swinging prior to the leader's grand entrance.

"Hey, Simon?" Ben called across the hall and Small sauntered down from the stage. "Who is the warm-up act, mate?"

Simon looked around, "Howie Morrison."

Ben blinked. "Sir Howard Morrison? You've got Sir Howard as the warm-up act? How did you pull that off? He hates Murdoch."

"Not Sir Howard. This is Howie Morrison. Looks and sounds just like him, though, with the help of a bit of make-up. He's on the party's electorate committee in Ashburton. Howie's a scream." Simon looked satisfied with himself.

"Let's get this straight, Simon," Ben said slowly. "To

launch the party's campaign for the election you're planning to put on stage, someone who will take the piss out of the most beloved entertainer in the country. Worse, the beloved entertainer is Maori, this galoot is pakeha. I'll lay you ten to one your Howie tells jokes about the Treaty. The next days the chooks will crucify us. The radio and the papers and the telly will say 'Murdoch backs racist attack on Kiwi icon' and you'll be up to your arse in complaints to the Race Relations Conciliator."

"Bloody media." Simon looked crestfallen. "The Conciliator is one of us, though, isn't he? We apppoint him don't we?"

"Howie has to go, Simon."

They finally decided on using more of the Maori concert party and Brenda provided an added boost by returning thirty minutes later, after scouring Cathedral Square, with a Pacific Island a capella group and a couple of athletic break-dancing youngsters who, she claimed, would add some street funk to the campaign launch.

To Simon Small's credit he auditioned Brenda's refugee artists and discovered the boys sang like angels and the dancers were capable of breathtaking gymnastics.

It worked.

Murdoch and Faith entered the hall to a thunderous haka from the concert party. There came a well-orchestrated standing ovation from the roaring crowd of well-heeled party supporters, who were even more excited by their unusually close proximity to a pair of gyrating street kids. The youngsters' flailing feet cleared the Murdochs a path down the packed aisle and the a capella group broke into a tear-inducing version of 'God Defend New Zealand'.

Ben's forecast was right. After an arrival that looked like

the Second Coming, Murdoch could have simply recited the stations on the main trunk line and he would have received tumultuous applause. As it was, the usual Murdoch platitudes were met with roars of approval, despite a puzzling ad lib reference to "a thousand points of brilliance" in the "history of our future".

"Dear God," Ben muttered and shook his head with bemusement as the cheering crowd clapped wildly.

"Prayers will not help, Bradshaw." Daniel McGrath was at his shoulder. "Even the Almighty would find it a big ask to save Murdoch's bum at this election."

"He is a cretin, isn't he, Danny?" Ben reverted to the endearing habit of ridiculing the Prime Minister more than the press gallery would. Most journalists were surprised to find themselves defending Murdoch to his own media strategist. It was a subtle way of forcing the hacks to look at the positives in Murdoch while allowing Ben to vent his spleen about his boss.

"Well," McGrath agreed, "he's never going to make Mensa."

"He's never going to make School Cert," said Ben glumly.

"Oh. He's not that dumb. I suppose you don't get to be leader of a party and Prime Minister if you're that stupid. He's got street smarts. Cunning."

Ben looked at him. "You really think so?"

"For sure. He's a cunning one, that Donald Murdoch." McGrath was practising his Irish accent.

"I suppose you're right." Ben shrugged as he waved farewell and headed backstage to where Murdoch had retired at the climactic end to the speech. "Murdoch's having a few drinks in his suite at the Park Royal later. See you up there."

Danny McGrath gave a little disco boogie, saying

sarcastically, "Ooh wee, that promises to be a wild and crazy night." Suddenly a rare thought struck him. "I don't suppose that young Brenda will be there?"

"You're disgusting, McGrath. She's young enough to be your niece."

A sly cackle was the only reply.

Later Ben would try to recall how the disaster occurred, but it was only near noon the next day on an inspection tour of an ostrich farm near Timaru, when Susan strolled along beside him, that he managed to piece it all together.

The first clue had come at around 7.15 am, when the phone rang shrilly beside his hotel bed and dimly, in his sleep, he came to the conclusion his right arm was paralysed. It rang a second time and he considered the possibility he had suffered a minor stroke. By the third ring he sensed the problem was a weight pressing his arm into the mattress. By the fourth he concluded the mass was warm and female.

It was on the fifth insistent peal of the phone that he put aside the hopeful thought it might have been Susan. His free hand subtly explored the obstruction and found its topography bore no resemblance to that of the woman he had briefly dreamed might be there.

His left arm found the phone and his right slipped out from beneath Brenda, a fact he confirmed with a quick peek. She was stirring.

"Go away. I'm dead. If I'm not, I soon will be," he whispered into the handset, gently pushing Brenda's head away from his chest.

"Murdoch here." The Prime Minister's voice ricocheted down the phone line. "I know you're alive," he barked. "Although Faith had her doubts after the amount of Cointreau you downed last night."

Ben tried to figure out if it was a migraine or simply a silent scream that pierced his head.

"Now, Ben, you've seen the papers, I suppose? What did you think of the interview on *Morning Report*? I thought I dealt with him quite effectively . . . Ben? You caught *Morning Report*?"

Brenda had been feigning sleep. Her teeth found his nipple. Ben gave a small yelp and pushed her head away forcefully. Sadly, the momentum sent her southward and his involuntary stiff intake of breath drew a rebuke from the Prime Minister, who took it as an admission of dereliction of duty.

"The cars leave in thirty minutes. You'd better not have a hangover. I need you in top form today, Ben."

He grunted a reply but Murdoch cut in, "Have you seen Brenda? Faith says she's not in her room. She must be having breakfast." Having answered his own question the Prime Minister slammed the phone down.

It took Ben three attempts before the receiver found the cradle and by that time Brenda had found something that intensely interested her under the covers.

"I have to shower," he said weakly. Her reply was incoherent and he surrendered.

The dapper grey-suited figure of Simon Small was anxiously pacing the lobby, pointedly pulling his sleeve up to reveal his garish gold watch, when Ben finally dragged his suitcase up to reception and paid the bill.

Through the lobby window he saw the swaying rear end of Brenda Murdoch bouncing out to the motorcade and Susan Lewis leaning on the far end of the desk giving him a long look.

He retrieved his gold American Express card and began

picking at the recesses of his mind, trying to establish in exact sequence the events of the night before. There were few clues as to what had led to the morning's nightmare scenario. He dismissed immediately all thoughts of the momentary weakness that overcame him around twenty past seven that morning and tried to recall what happened several hours earlier.

Sweeping past Susan with a fast, "Hi! How are ya, gotta go," he glanced at the receipt and realised that, whatever had happened, his mini-bar had taken an awful toll. The party paid for the room plus 'actual and reasonable' expenses. The party mandarins might regard $220 as an actual but certainly unreasonable expense.

Halfway to the ostrich farm, somewhere on the long straight road south, a wave of nausea was accompanied by the memory of Daniel McGrath being carried from his suite by Susan and a couple of other journalists. However, the exact circumstances that led Brenda into his bed remained obscure.

"You win Best Party of the Campaign Trail award, Benny," said Susan as she pouted through the fence at a bird that pouted back.

Ben grunted. The best defence against her curiosity was to play dumb, but she was not prepared to let the matter go.

"So?" A simple word that was both a question and a statement.

Ben grunted again.

"How did you and Brenda get on after the boys and I decided to rid your room of the disgusting McGrath?"

"Ah," drawled Ben, realising evasion seemed called for. "What did you do with Danny?"

"We took him downstairs and propped him up on a

couch. He didn't have a room at the hotel and no one knew where he was staying. Just as well, really. He was still sitting there this morning, fast asleep, so at least he didn't miss the cars when they left. The *Press* photographer gave him a lift. He's still comatose in the back seat."

Ben quickened his pace to try to catch up with the Prime Minister's group several metres ahead but Susan grabbed his sleeve. "So, Benny, how did you get her out of your bed? She crashed there shortly after we arrived back from Murdoch's room? Remember?"

He assured her he recalled the events of the night perfectly and Brenda had been no trouble.

"Ain't that the truth," she said waspishly, striding off.

Ben thought he detected eerie echoes of one of his ex-wives in that parting crack and he decided that he was well rid of her for the moment. The media posse caught up and passed him. Brenda gave a cute five-fingered wave as she coasted by.

Dear Lord, he thought miserably, can there be anything as vile as four weeks on the road?

9

The Spin

A couple of days later Ben decided televised leaders' debates were definitely worse that any other part of the campaign.

The hour or more in a hot studio or some draughty town hall under bright television lights was the easy part. It was tension of the build-up to the television showdown. All the leaders knew the importance of the debates. In a culture driven by an illuminated tube it was a truism that the telly could make or break a political career.

Nelson Mandela only became President of South Africa because he had spent most of his political life behind bars, locked away from *60 Minutes*, CNN and the nightly news. He spoke too slowly for a good sound bite, he thought too long and seriously for a slick retort in studio argument, he cared too deeply to be glib under journalistic cross-examination and he looked too old to be truly credible in an increasingly youth-oriented society.

Winnie Mandela, on the other hand, apart from the occasional banning order and bout of house arrest, was long exposed to the laser-sharp surgical heat of the media machine. It carefully built her up and tore her down while Nelson was safely insulated on Robben Island, ruminating on post-Apartheid social policies in his cell.

Television had not been kind to Murdoch. It was a medium better designed for a man like Christopher Cross with his youthful chiselled good looks, smart mouth and flashes of quick humour. While Richard Foot's political day had largely come and gone, the Liberal leader had been a child of the television age and his carefully tailored one-liners were calculated to score points. Even a left-wing dinosaur like Paul Knox came across as sincere because he was. There had to be some small advantage in honesty.

By contrast, Murdoch appeared lumbering and slow-witted. It was like watching your father compete on *Mastermind*. Ben hoped there would be some sympathy vote from his leader's wallowing effort.

"Prime Minister, so good to see you. I tell you, Don, you've waged one hell of a campaign so far." The dapper little man in the Armani suit had Murdoch by the arm and was propelling him to the studio's green room couch.

"I only launched it three days ago, mate," said Murdoch, casting his eyes around for a drink.

"And every day a master stroke, may I say. A series of master strokes, Don." Mr Armani patted Murdoch's knee. He had a knack of achieving instant familiarity. Some people would describe it as crawling, but in the television industry it was called schmoozing and was simply accepted practice. Television was, Ben thought, the only business more amoral than politics.

"Now, Don, remember we don't have a lot of time tonight. So, ah . . . we'll need to you be brief and to the point." Murdoch's long-windedness was legend among television interviewers.

"The Prime Minister would like a scotch. Johnny Walker. Black Label," Ben announced.

The man in the Armani barely glanced up. "Of course you would, Don. I'll see if I can rustle one up. They're not big on it around here. I'll see if they can find some."

He stood and threw a look at Ben. "Just a small one, I think."

They walked off together, the interviewer looking back at Murdoch leafing through some notes.

"Jesus, Ben. He reeks of it. How many has he had?"

"Don't you worry. It's not your problem." Ben and he had

a long friendship going back many years. An unusual feat in the vanity-ridden world of broadcasting.

"It will be if he chunders in the middle of the debate. Or worse, throws up on my new threads," said the interviewer, fingering his lapel. "Seriously, he's OK? Remember that interview we did with him by satellite from New York? I could only use a couple of minutes of it. He was out to lunch."

"Well," said Ben firmly. "Tonight he is definitely in for dinner. He'll make a meal of these turkeys but he needs a couple of shots to fire him up. Dead cold sober, Donald Murdoch would have your audience sleeping in the aisles."

He wandered back to the couch and sat beside Murdoch.

"Remember, Cross is the one. Concentrate only on him." Ben felt like an All Black coach drilling the team before an Eden Park test. "Be as pleasant as you can to Knox and Foot. You may need them after the election and, besides, they don't count for anything. People don't care about them. It's Cross you want. He's portrayed as the giant-killer. People want to see you take him out . . . or him take you out."

Ben looked up and saw Chris making his usual late entrance. He clapped an arm around the Armani and waved across at Foot on the other side of the green room. Cross moved to talk to the Liberal leader and his advisors for a few minutes before striding over to see Paul Knox, who was sitting alone, watching the end of the news on a television set in the corner.

"Look at the bastards. They've already cut their cosy little deal," Murdoch rumbled. A producer arrived with the drink and Murdoch abruptly stood and sauntered towards Cross, who turned and faced him.

"You'll need a few more of those, Don, before the evening's out," said Cross with a knowing smirk.

"Said your prayers tonight?" snapped Murdoch. "Or maybe you've gone off saying them."

Subtle as a brick through a window, Ben muttered to himself, steering himself between the two men.

Cross was flushed. Knox was pointedly ignoring the confrontation, staring at the television. On the other side of the green room Richard Foot and his scrum of advisors tittered amongst themselves.

"You're the one who hasn't got a prayer, Murdoch. You are finished and you and your cronies know it," Christopher Cross hissed.

"Kiss my arse, Cross."

"Go fuck yourself, Murdoch."

"Oh, good. An intellectual debate. I love it." The interviewer sped across from the door. "I think it is time we went through to the studio."

This should be good, Ben decided.

He watched the debate on a monitor in another room upstairs, where several press gallery correspondents had camped. Murdoch retained his balance for much of the show, getting in a couple of hard blows against Cross when the Freedom Party leader showed a lack of detailed policy on an issue. The remainder of the time he needled him. By contrast, Murdoch was almost absurdly deferential and polite to the two other leaders. For their part, the other three hacked at each other remorselessly, each attempting to appear the one and true opposition party.

"Is Murdoch holding out an olive branch to Foot?" Daniel McGrath asked.

Ben shrugged. "Maybe you could say that. Certainly Cross hasn't got Foot locked up, or Knox for that matter. That's the problem with any centre-left coalition. They all distrust each other. In some ways, the other parties prefer the Government as the devil they know. I'm not saying Murdoch would seek a deal with any of them, but they all know he is a man they can deal with if they have to."

The seeds of the next day's headlines had been sown. Tomorrow's papers would speculate on a breach between Freedom and the Liberals, hinting either might do an about face and come to a post election arrangement with Murdoch. It would make them look more unstable and unreliable while promoting the Conservative Government as more tenable.

As Ben had planned, Murdoch bounded out of the studio first, claiming victory to the journalists who crowded around. By the time Cross, Foot and Knox appeared they were put in the position of denying Murdoch's self-proclaimed victory and rebutting suggestions of an irretrievable rift between their parties. The latter was a position none of them relished stating: it was in each party's interest to appear independent, willing and capable of leading a majority Government in its own right.

Political reality, however, dictated differently and they would almost certainly have to come to some agreement if any of them was to occupy the Treasury benches. Consequently they had to appear to both like and dislike each other. It was a tough act that did not appear really credible.

While they struggled to retrieve the lost ground, Murdoch and his team were on the road again.

"Did you see the bastards back-pedalling there, Ben?" The Prime Minister was still in the first flush of post debate euphoria. "It was the same right through the debate. They spent so much time hacking away at each other I could sit back and score at will."

He had convinced himself he had won a major victory. Ben was not keen on disabusing him of the notion – it would build his confidence for the rest of the campaign.

In fact, while Murdoch had not been embarrassed or wrong-footed during the show, he had failed to say anything of real substance. All crust and no pie, thought the strategist. Still, that was Murdoch and if he failed to deliver much in the way of detail at least the public would find little to be offended by in what he said.

"You nailed Cross nicely on the Treaty settlement," Ben said. Murdoch twisted around in his seat and grinned.

"He wanted to play the race card. He can pay the price. It's all very well to oppose the Waitangi Tribunal but it is impossible for someone like him to come up with a realistic alternative. What do you do? Let Maori grievances fester and blight the future of the next generation?"

Again, without realising it, Murdoch was quoting Ben's words back to him from a speech he had crafted a couple of years before. The Prime Minister had a sponge-like ability to absorb a good line and make it his own.

"What puzzles me, Ben, is how he attracts so much Maori support."

"Simple, boss. They recognise his expediency and think they can turn it to their advantage. They believe they can manoeuvre him into a position where they can turn back on the tap to access more tax revenues for Maori development through a reconstituted Maori Affairs Department while still maintaining a degree of Treaty settlements."

"They'll rue the day they trusted Christopher Cross," Murdoch sneered. "Believe me, Ben, those Maori boys don't know what they've got themselves into."

Paternalistic and patronising Murdoch might be on the

question of Maori and Treaty issues, but he remained vaguely honourable in his dealing with them.

"Actually, PM, I think a few Maori might be waking up to Cross. I saw Luke Watene a while back. He didn't seem to be brimming with goodwill toward his party leader." Ben ruminated on the passing meeting they had in the waterfront bar in Wellington. Cross had basically snubbed Watene and in front of his own circle of friends there that night Watene seemed to be almost sneering at Chris.

Murdoch watched the lights of Queen Street flash past and waved to a group of people who recognised him. They seemed to be shouting something, most likely abuse.

"What do you make of Knox?" Murdoch suddenly asked.

For a moment Ben was at a loss. The Socialist leader was an enigma, a strong, caring man with a total belief in himself who had been so bereft at his wife's sudden and tragic death that it appeared for a while as if he might throw in politics. As time went on, however, it seemed to make him stronger, more resolute.

This was, probably, the last effect anyone would have wanted it to have on Paul Knox, who was already somewhat inflexible on matters of doctrine. He ruled the Socialist party by the sheer force of his own iron will. The public had an impression of him as a soft, almost gentle man. Instead, those who knew him behind the Socialist Party scenes could testify to the fact he had a vitriolic tongue and an implacable hatred of anyone perceived as an enemy.

Sadly, Knox had an uncanny knack of being able to create foes out of friends. Any poor unfortunate who crossed him, even once, would find themselves a pariah, frozen out of the party. Consquently, the list of refugees and exiles from the Socialist party was almost as long as its current membership.

He was also a total believer in the doctrine that the ends justified the means. So certain was he of the correctness of his mission that virtually any subterfuge or deception was permissible when it came to advancing the cause of the party. This earned him a reputation of complete untrustworthiness amongst those opposition parties that might otherwise have considered a post election alliance with the Socialists.

Not that Knox or his key party loyalists necessarily wanted one. They had the classic left's long-term vision of history and were prepared to spend a decade, or however long it might take, in the wilderness to gain power. Absolute power was the only thing they aspired to, for that meant they would have to make no compromises once elected. Their agenda was as rigid as they were and their consciences, such as they were, would not allow them the slightest deviation from their principles. To be honest, they preferred not being in government. That way they were spared the difficult concessions running the country would require them to make.

None of this would be of any interest to Murdoch, so Ben simply speculated that one of Knox's MPs was enjoying a dramatic rise to dominance in the Socialist Party and was becoming a potential threat to Knox's continued leadership after the election. This was mainly due to the fact the rival's brother was having a wild affair with the feminist icon who the Socialist Party's president. The Prime Minister grunted with satisfaction. He understood the fear of a leadership challenge and relished the gossip about illicit sex.

"Those lefties are all the same, Ben. Like bloody rabbits. They just can't keep it zipped up. Can you imagine our esteemed party president rogering anyone? Say, you reckon you could drop the news to the chooks?" Murdoch inquired idly.

"That's where I got it from, Prime Minister."

"Oh. They always protect those people. That's because they're at it themselves. Like that Lewis woman and Cross."

"Perhaps," ventured Ben. "Perhaps they don't believe a politician's sexual predilections have anything to do with the way he does his job."

Murdoch snorted with derision and they drove the rest of the way in silence.

In a private reception room at a downtown hotel the Prime Minister and several of his staff mingled with business leaders invited to discuss the campaign's progress. Most had a vested interest in it as they were large contributors to the party coffers.

Several of the businessmen congregated around Murdoch, who was adamantly assuring them that the sale of the Energy Corporation would not be the last great asset sale. The Government simply had to downplay the question of further sales for the time being. He pointed out that selling Energy so close to the election had proved a bad blow to the Government, reviving public interest in the sales issue, depressing its poll ratings.

"It was a mistake. The timing of the sale so close to the campaign. No doubt about that and I will take responsibility for the decision," he conceded before immediately trying to shirk responsibility for it. "You must realise there are those in my Cabinet who hold to a very hard line. Ruled by doctrine. They told me we couldn't afford to be seen to back down on the Energy sale. No U-turns, we'd be crucified, they said. Ha!" He gave an explosive snort. "We were bloody crucified anyway."

Incited by conspiracy theorists like Christopher Cross out in the misty wastes of talkback radioland, many people seriously believed big-business interests ran the nation, using men like Murdoch as their stooges. The reality was far more mundane. The corporates lobbied the politicians mercilessly on occasions such as this, waving their company donations to the party's funds, but their attempts at applying pressure failed more often than not. The politicians realised, whatever business may demand, policy changes still had to be sold to a not entirely stupid public who had a lot more votes than a few fat and greedy businessmen.

People prefered to believe in conspiracies. If they were weak or poor, if they felt they were losers or insecure, it was easier to blame their misfortunes on villains like a big-business cabal rather than any failings of their own.

Across the room, near the bar, Ben and party president Ernie Watts stood talking with Clarry Evans.

Watts watched Murdoch's nervous movements. "He never feels comfortable with these people, does he?"

Clarry clamped his teeth on the end of his cigar and drawled, "That's because he thinks they despise him."

"They do," said Ben.

Watts and Evans laughed.

"True," agreed Clarry. "They really do find him a bit, ah, dull. Well, to be honest, they think he's a bit thick. Still, they don't have to love him, just fund him. They haven't got a lot of choice, anyway. He's Prime Minister. He's leader of the governing party, which happens to be their kind of party."

"And if they want a knighthood, they have to play along with him. What's the going rate on a knighthood these days, Clarry?" Ben asked.

Clarry Evans tutted and winked. "That's very cynical, Ben."

"About two hundred grand," said Simon Small, who had

edged his way into their group.

"Now, Simon, obviously being a donor to the party is not going to hurt, but you need a lot more credentials than that for an honour like a knighthood," Evans said, grinning.

The Prime Minister's hatchet man snorted. "I try to tell those silly buggers every time they try and scrap the knighthoods. Who the hell's going to pay good money for an Order of the Tuatara or some other God awful Kiwi medallion?"

"There's more to getting a knighthood than money," Clarry insisted, tapping his ash into a pot plant on the kauri table behind him.

"Yes. You're right," said Ben. "You have to get your mates, who are preferably already knights themselves, to write to the Government and write to everyone else they can think of with any power and lobby like Christ." He warmed to his theme. "A good reputation, good connections and a couple of hundred grand should see you right, Sir Simon."

Small bristled. "Knighthoods don't mean a thing to me."

"Ah, but they might to Lady Small," Clarry Evans put in wickedly and Simon flinched.

"Imagine if we lost the election," mused Ben. "No honours, no appointments to Government boards and committees, no one seeking us out for our opinion. We'd be almost like real people, Clarry."

"Wash your mouth out, Ben." Evans shuddered theatrically.

"And go rescue your boss from his corporate allies before each starts telling what they really think of the other."

Back at the hotel, finally escaping yet another post-mortem of the televison debate in the Prime Minister's room after yet another scotch, Ben made his way down to the bar.

As usual, Susan was sitting in the corner, drink in hand, her back to the wall so she could keep an eye on the room.

"People-watching," she replied when Ben asked her how she had spent the evening.

He noticed her cellphone on the table beside her and wondered whether she had spoken to Cross tonight. She read his thoughts.

"That little toad will be here in a minute. In fact" – she looked at the gold Cartier – "he was due here half an hour ago."

"So much for keeping his distance during the campaign," Ben said under his breath.

A small stir in the lobby signalled Chris's arrival. The doorman snapped to attention, heads turned at the reception desk, couples stood back to let him pass. At the entrance to the bar Tony, one of the patrolling DPS guards, paused, winked at Ben and made the sign of the cross.

Chris swept past the policeman with barely a glance in his direction. When he walked Chris moved at great speed, giving the impression of a man with considerable momentum both physically and politically. Which made it all the more surprising that he was habitually late for appointments.

The fast pace was part of the Cross act, designed to promote the energetic image of a busy man going places. The tardiness was a measure of his arrogance and a device carefully calculated to ensure he received the maximum attention. No one took any notice of the first person to enter a room because there was no audience. A late arrival guaranteed a crowd and the chances were those waiting would have had plenty of time to talk about him.

He smiled his famous crooked smile at Susan who, Ben was appalled to see, positively blossomed in its radiance.

"You blokes ready to raise the white flag yet, Ben?" He lowered himself into an armchair opposite.

"Yes, the entire Government is now prepared to surrender, Chris."

"Did you see the poll tonight? Freedom's bounced back to 22 percent. You guys have run aground and are stuck fast on 35 percent. My own polling shows us much higher, around the 30 percent mark, and you guys losing more ground." Opinion polls had the same effect as Prozac on Chris's nervous system.

"Chris," said Ben huffily, "don't bullshit me. You guys can't afford polls. I hear you've got a couple of businesses to agree to tack some attitudinal questions about political parties on the end of their own market research but they are in no way as accurate as the proper voter polls run by the media and our own people."

Cross snorted and clicked his fingers at a waiter. If anyone else snapped their fingers at bar staff they would probably die of dehydration, but Cross had a large whisky magically appear on the table in front of him.

Despite Ben's denials, Cross had struck a nerve with his crack about the Government's poll ratings. Once into an election period Governments seldom, if ever, improved their standing. Murdoch's party had slumped several points in the run-up to the campaign and there seemed little hope of recovering as the weight of campaign propaganda tended to be anti-government in nature.

The Government's only hope was a small scheme Ben had hatched a few months before with the same cadre of businessmen Murdoch had dined with tonight. The businessmen would run a sizable advertising campaign ostensibly targeted at praising the economy and encouraging investment. Because the commercials and newspaper ads never mentioned the Conservative Party they would not count as election spending or be subject to the bureaucratic rules that restricted the amount of television time available to the parties.

In an election a government faced several opposition parties united in one thing only, their combined criticism of the policies of the ruling party. Ben felt his small deal with the Conservatives' big-business backers helped redress that imbalance, effectively doubling the amount of positive advertising for the Government.

The deal had not come without a price. The businessmen had insisted on the Energy Corporation sale proceeding as a measure of the Government's commitment to the free market / less government cause. The net effect had been to create a minor backlash from the public, who deeply resented foreign commercial interests gaining control of such assets. What the Government gained in extra advertising was probably lost in the negative attitudes created by the sale.

Cross was, himself, briskly dismissive of the businessmen's ads. "They can waste their money if they like. They're paying a fortune for television time. I'm getting it for free. I've had the last two weeks out on the road, scoring story after story on the television news while Murdoch waited too late to launch his own. Why the hell did you guys wait so long?"

"Well, you know Murdoch, Chris. He's too damned over-confident. He thought all we needed was a short, sharp campaign." Ben looked around fruitlessly for the waiter. "Who else wants a drink?"

Cross snapped the magic fingers and a man appeared within seconds.

The drinks proved a good distraction. Chris had been trying to resolve some nagging doubts he had about the timing of his campaign versus the Government's apparent lethargic start.

What Cross had not figured out was the all-important allocation of news time on the state-owned television networks. Ben had. To ensure absolute fairness, the mandarins of broadcasting applied a stopwatch to their news shows. They would assess how much time, right down to the last second, had been allocated to each of the major parties in every bulletin and try and ensure they were balanced by the election day.

By launching himself a fortnight early Cross might have got a lot more news time in the first couple of weeks of the campaign, but now that Murdoch had formally begun his own push to retain power, Chris was about to find Freedom's coverage would shrink. If Ben was correct in his thinking, the overall effect should be to have Murdoch suddenly climb into prominence while giving the appearance that Cross was fading away in the couple of weeks that remained before polling day. It was a sneaky trick but it was legal.

Cross was suspicious but had not yet realised what was about to happen. Ben could hear his wail of anguish when he realised he was no longer getting much coverage on the news programmes.

"Ah, Chris, I guess you just outsmarted us yet again," sighed Ben, who leaned back on the couch beside Susan.

"You're up to something, buddy. I've got my eye on you," Cross warned with a laugh. He was making subtle eye-contact with Susan and Ben wondered about the hidden signals being exchanged. "Anyway." Cross gulped his drink. It seemed the signals had been successfully decoded and the lovers were about to adjourn to somewhere less public.

"How do you reckon the debate went, Chris?" Ben was being mildly malicious, delaying the departure. He felt Susan's foot strike his ankle.

"I won." Modesty was not Christopher Cross's strong suit. "Knox came out looking like Lenin on speed. Foot looked like the tawdry old hack he is. Your man Murdoch need not have come at all. All he did was mouth the usual platitudes. Who does he think he's fooling?"

Ben ignored Susan, who was ostentatiously picking up her bag and looking at her watch. "I thought he came back quite strongly on the Treaty issue. You must be shedding some Maori support if you continue to slam the Waitangi Tribunal, the Maori business leadership and the radicals?"

"They'll stick with me, Buddy. You can't label me a racist." Cross had slipped into a favourite election speech. "So I talk about a New Zealand for New Zealanders. What's wrong with that? I'm opposed to selling out to foreign interests. The Maori know the dangers of letting foreign interests gain control, believe me, that's the lesson of history that the Maori have learned. As for the Waitangi Tribunal and the Treaty settlements, your ordinary Maori guy in the street hasn't seen one red cent in all these years of waiting. What they need is what they once had, a strong Department of Maori Affairs and some big targeted funding for economic development."

Cross clicked his fingers one last time for the bill.

"You told that to guys like Luke Watene and Willy Ihaka? They're your candidates aren't they? I'm not sure they'd be going along with you on that one," Ben probed gently.

"I make the policy in this party." Chris looked at the

drinks bill, reached into his pocket and pulled out a fifty-dollar note. "Bugger Luke Watene and fat cats like Ihaka. They think they run the party's Maori policy. They don't. The day after we become the Government the Maori policy goes back into the hands of the common Maori people, not some self-appointed brown elite." Cross nodded at the waiter. "Keep the change."

Susan had wandered over to the lift. Cross muttered a goodbye to Ben and strolled after her. When the lift doors closed on the couple Ben turned back to the waiter idly cleaning the table.

"Nice to see you again, Freddy. How's your brother getting on?"

The waiter looked up and grinned at the recognition.

"Long time no see, Benny. Yeah, Luke's fine. Just fine and he's not keen on being buggered, I can tell you."

They both began laughing.

"Cheers, Fred. Hope the law degree goes well, although with the hours you're working I don't know where you get the time to study."

"Oh, you know us self-appointed elite, Ben. We pay someone else to do the studying for us, don't we?" The young man laughed again.

"Give my regards to Luke when you next speak to him," Ben called over his shoulder as he left.

"Oh, indeed I will, Ben."

10
The Spin

They flew out at the dawn the next morning, Murdoch's leased turbo-prop clawing itself to higher altitude over the Waikato.

In the back row of the plane Susan Lewis sat with her head on the seat-back, eyes closed. Ben could see the tiny patterns the dark veins traced on the pale lids.

"Stop staring. It isn't polite. I haven't got my war paint on yet, Ben," Susan groaned, her eyes still shut.

"You are so beautiful, to me," he crooned softly.

One eye opened. "You never give up, do you? What time is it? It's barely dawn and you're trying to seduce me."

Ben shrugged.

"Oh, you are a darling, Ben." She sighed in exasperation. "As opposed to Mr Wham Bam Thank You, Ma'am. I think I know why they call him Speedy."

"Ah. Chris didn't stay long, I gather?"

"No. To put it crudely, he came and went. Shortly after midnight he turned into a pumpkin. Why am I so attracted to bastards?" she asked.

"Now, that is a not uncommon syndrome among women," Ben advised her. "In fact, I put my own considerable success down to that bastard factor."

She put her hand on his. "You're not a bastard."

"Give me the chance," he implored and Susan began laughing.

"I couldn't take you away from Brenda," she teased. "How is the little dear?"

"God, don't ask me. I think she may have made the ultimate sacrifice for the good of the party with Danny McGrath last night."

Susan peered over the seat in front, trying to spot the girl. "That's above and beyond the call of duty, Ben."

"It's dirty work but someone has to do it."

They were still giggling and chatting amiably when the plane touched down in Napier. On the tarmac Simon Small stood by the limo. He was acting as the party's advance man that day.

Murdoch strode down the steps and, sensing local photographers closing in for a shot, he cast around and seized Small's hand, pumping it furiously while he grinned at the lens. Small glared malevolently at the press.

"Mmmm. You give good handshake, Simon," purred Susan as she skipped by.

"He has to have a handshake, Simon. You know the rules. He lands. He disembarks. He shakes someone's hand." Ben hissed at Simon in Simon's ear. "You should have lined up the mayor. What's the betting *Metro* will now get hold of that picture and subtitle it, 'Prime Minister Murdoch and a visitor from Hawke's Bay'?"

"How was I to know? That girl Julie in your office should have arranged it," cried Small as he struggled along in the party's wake.

"You're the advance man, Simon. You're in charge. Murdoch has to have something to do with his hands otherwise he starts pointing and waving wildly at the cameras and anyone else who strays near. Better have a handshake lined up by the time we get over to Hastings." Ben slammed the limo door and the Prime Minister's car sped off across the airport, sandwiched between two police escort cars.

Small flung his hands in the air and ran for his rental car outside the terminal. The reporters had already hurled themselves into their own vehicles and a campaign mini-bus.

Often the departure of the Prime Minister was marked by a mad scramble and Le Mans-style racing start as the PM's staff, the media and the police jostled for position in the motorcade.

In the lead LTD Murdoch was beginning to enjoy the campaign trail. "Right, Ben. What's on the agenda?"

"Let's see. Holland Road Primary School. Principal Mrs Davies. She's friendly enough by all accounts. The staff aren't a hotbed of radicalism, although they all went on strike the last time the NZEI took them out." Ben leafed through the folder on his knee.

"Ah, yes. They have a new gym and school hall. The schedule is as follows . . . Tour gym and hall, school choir sings 'Blowing in the Wind', inspect classroom computer studies, then tea and a chat with the staff."

Murdoch grunted and Ben went on. "They have an innovative computer teaching programme which fits nicely with our Learning in the Twenty-First Century policy programme. We've got a television ad on that theme which starts screening tonight and for the rest of the week. The coverage of you checking out the school's computers and the kids should dovetail nicely. Overall issues here are . . ." He ferreted deeper in the file. "Issues are teacher-pupil ratios which are running a little higher here than many other regions. Some staff retention difficulties. I suspect the big one, of course, will be pay parity."

Murdoch groaned. "Let's have a look at the figures on staff-pupil ratios." He reached over for the papers and Ben passed another slim sheaf of documents with the school's details.

"There's some additional background there on Maori preschool funding. We'll also have to have a trot through the kohanga reo next door. Make it quick there. We've short-changed the kohanga reos a couple of years in a row and it could get ugly. Besides, the kaumatua will be out in force and we don't want to get slowed down in an hour-long powhiri."

Murdoch's head whipped around. "Find out who's going to be there. I smell an ambush."

He was right, Ben thought. Simon had not attached a list of Maori dignitaries likely to attend.

"What follows all this?" Murdoch demanded.

"Ah, local radio station. Interview and talkback. Private station. Young woman interviewer. I've checked her out, she should be a pussycat. Then onto the vineyard for lunch. Big issue there will be the wine tariffs."

"Too high or too low?" the Prime Minister wanted to know.

"Too low. Too much foreign competition. They'll also want some assurances we'll help them in their battle with the European Community's wine commissars, who are trying to drive them out of business by insisting they own the copyright to virtually every name of every variety of wine ever produced. They probably think they even own the name 'wine'."

"Do we want to help them?"

"We do. Within limits."

"Faith likes a glass of wine, don't you, dear?" It was more a question than a statement by Murdoch. Ben was mildly surprised that Murdoch appeared to have missed noticing what his wife drank over the past couple of decades.

However, Faith was unfazed. "Dry white, darling. A Sauvignon Blanc if they have it." She sounded a little distracted, as if she was ordering a glass.

"Um. That will be a little later, Mrs Murdoch. Over lunch," Ben tentatively put in.

"Oh, of course, Benny. I was daydreaming."

Murdoch's eyes rolled and, as they pulled up to the school's administration block, he grabbed the door handle and prepared to propel himself out of the car.

"Don't move too quickly!" Ben warned urgently. "The cameras are in cars following us."

It was too late. Murdoch was gone, the door slamming behind him as the car slid to a halt. A melee developed as the media dumped their vehicles in the driveway and raced to follow him.

While the school choir demanded to know exactly how many roads a man must walk down, Ben was outside yelling into a cellphone at Simon Small.

"Surely you have to know who is going to be in the welcoming party at the kohanga reo? For all you know it could be the whole Moutoa Gardens branch of Black Power!"

He cut off Simon's bleating protestations that it was, once again, Julie's fault and stomped across the rough dry turf of the football field to the block of prefabs that housed the Maori preschool.

"Kia ora, Luke! How did I know you'd be here?" he laughed as a young Maori man in a well-cut blue suit stood up from the bench outside the classroom.

"Hey, Ben! Didn't you know I was on the board of trustees?"

Luke Watene was a handsome man in his mid thirties. There were still traces of his hard youth in his face. A glint of an unspoken challenge in the eyes. The laughter lines tempered by creases of wariness. A small tattoo of a stylised bird poked out from under the cuff of a starched white shirt.

He had gone from adolescent gangs into political activism, which, in turn, led him to university and ultimately a law degree. The explosive growth of tribally based Maori business brought about by the Treaty settlement process had taken him naturally to a position of prominence within his own iwi. From there it had been a short step into politics. He was now the Freedom Party's candidate for the Eastern Maori seat and, in the Byzantine way Maori politics works, had been anointed by various hui as the favoured person to win the seat.

He shook Ben firmly by the hand before pulling him closer to hongi, foreheads lightly touching, their breath mingling. Ben reminded himself to warn the Prime Minister again of the delicacy of the traditional greeting. The pressing of noses was an act Murdoch invariably botched. Some ancient Celtic instinct in him tended to treat it more like a Liverpool kiss.

"You're on the board of trustees here?" Ben asked as they parted.

"Nah, over at the school, but my iwi trust board is heavily involved here."

Ben thought for a moment. "You don't even come from around here, do you?"

Luke smiled. "These are my mother's people."

"Whatever." Ben waved his arms. "We have a problem, Luke. We can't let you hijack the PM's visit for the Freedom Party."

Luke slipped into mocking street-talk. "S'all right, bro. You won't have no problem from these Maoris. That's why I'm here. Tell him I'll make sure the mokopuna don't bite."

He explained he was there purely as a member of the iwi's trust board and, to avoid any potential for controversy, he would personally escort Murdoch into the kohanga reo. Ben was relieved. Under Luke's guidance they could step through the minefield of Maori protocol that privately terrified Pakeha politicians like Murdoch and himself.

Luke gestured magnanimously. "You can sell it to the media as a genuinely bipartisan occasion. I will even generously compliment your man on his accomplishments in Maori education."

"What you want, Luke?" said Ben flatly.

"Nothing. I might need a favour from you folks one day. Besides, it makes me look good. I can't see any of your old tame Uncle Tom Conservative Party Maori rushing over here to look after the Prime Minister."

Ben agreed that was a bit of an oversight and made a mental note to have Simon Small killed. Perhaps only maimed. He was still weighing up the options when he saw the Prime Minister's group, surrounding by a flying wedge of cameras, leave the school staff-room and set out across the field.

"I better go and warn him. Thanks for your help."

"No problems, brother." Luke waved him away.

Ben turned, suddenly struck by a thought.

"I saw your brother last night in Auckland."

The man nodded. "I know. He told me."

Twenty-four hours later, over dinner in another hotel in yet another city, Susan Lewis described the school visit as the first real public-relations triumph scored by the Government in the entire campaign.

"I heard you say that on radio this afternoon," Ben mumbled through a forkful of Beef Wellington. "Why do you think it was so great?"

Susan shrugged. "Maybe because it was natural. For the

first time in this campaign something was real. The rest of this photo opportunity stuff is just junk. So sterile. Those kids yesterday, though, were great. The Maori stuff was a master stroke. How on earth did you get Luke Watene to lead him onto the marae and shepherd Murdoch through the welcome?"

Murdoch's discomfort at being confronted with a different culture inevitably showed and his embarrassment usually manifested itself in an appallingly patronising manner. He had been known to drop in a colloquial Maori accent on such occasions and Ben was always petrified his Prime Minister might conclude a marae speech with the phrase, "Eh, Boy?"

Thankfully, the Hawke's Bay kohanga reo visit proved utterly different. Watene's grace and easy manner rubbed off on the Prime Minister, who acquitted himself with unusual dignity.

The Hawke's Bay leg had turned into a minor publicity triumph. Most of the following day's papers carried prominent pictures of Murdoch being mobbed by small Maori children. Both channels' evening news bulletins concentrated heavily on the bipartisan aspect of the visit, which gave Murdoch another chance to launch into his 'We are One Nation. Two Peoples. Together We Embrace the Twenty-first Century' speech.

Simon Small had been livid. His focus group research continued to show Murdoch was identified as being soft on Maori issues and the angle the media took on the Napier visit simply reinforced this negative image, he argued. However, he was still in disgrace for his organisational failures in that visit and Murdoch was coasting happily on the respect he had been shown by the kaumatua and children. Small's criticisms had been loftily dismissed by the Prime Minister.

"I wish I could say it was all a result of my masterful election strategy. Truth is, we fluked it." Ben told Susan. He realised he was probably giving away too much and glanced away to wave cheerily at Brenda, who was gliding through the restaurant with her Walkman on. This was a mistake, as she interpreted the diversionary greeting as a sign of renewed lust and bounded across to their table.

Ben thought he could hear Susan's teeth grinding as Brenda breathlessly imparted her feelings on the campaign to date. "Overall, the old duffer's just too boring. Why doesn't he go to a student sit-in or something?" she asked.

"Perhaps because they're protesting against him, Brenda darling," Susan said stiffly.

"Oh."

"Hang on. That's not an altogether silly suggestion," drawled Ben.

Susan looked at him with stunned amazement.

Murdoch needed to appear strong, Ben thought. It was risky but a confrontation with students protesting Education spending cuts could work if it was controlled properly. Few New Zealanders attended university. Most people thought students were cosseted, privileged brats.

Murdoch did not even risk losing substantial student votes. The image of students as radicals was wrong. Generally they came from somewhat affluent backgrounds and were more conservative than their historically liberal baby-boomer parents. Anyway, the party polled well among eighteen- to twenty-nine-year-olds and it was unlikely to shed this support if Murdoch had a head-banging match with some protestors. Older voters might positively approve.

Kiwis love a strong leader. Facing down the students in their lair would be perceived as courageous. Ben did not bother to share this with Susan for she would almost certainly use the information to discredit the event. Let her work it out for herself, he thought, if she can.

"I'll think about it," he said to Brenda, who beamed and flashed a 'nah, nah, nah' look at the older woman across the table.

"Gee, I guess it will save the students burning him in effigy. They can use the real thing," Susan said drily, reaching for a glass of Sauvignon Blanc.

"Well, we need something," Brenda went on. "Danny told me this afternoon he had a big story that was going to blow our campaign wide apart. That's why he isn't down here in the restaurant or bar. He's filing the story for tomorrow's paper."

The well-worn alarm bells started ringing again for Ben. If McGrath was bypassing drinks, food and a luscious young woman with a pierced navel he must be onto a good story.

"Why don't you see if you can find out what it is, Brenda?" he suggested.

"OK." She bobbed up out of her seat and set off for McGrath's room.

Ben could picture the sight that would greet her upstairs. The atmosphere in the room would be thick with cigarette smoke and the floor would be spread with the detritus of McGrath's battered suitcase: old underwear, shirts, socks, newspapers and press statements. On the table beside the bed a laptop computer and modem would be plugged into the phone socket, a drink beside it and a trail of damp towels would mark his earlier path from the bathroom. Reporters lived like pigs. Someone who often described himself as an anal retentive, Ben found the whole scenario a horror.

"I should worry about what McGrath might have, but you never know whether our dear Brenda has got the right story or not. Is that girl simple, stoned or what?" Susan demanded. "I know she's Murdoch's niece and having Forrest Gump as an uncle would explain at lot but, Ben, with Brenda there is plenty of room upstairs for dancing, isn't there?"

"This from an otherwise intelligent woman who flagellates herself in a hopeless relationship with a congenital cheat?" Ben was peeved. It might have been her cheap shot about Don Murdoch's intelligence but he suspected it went deeper than that. He had no real attachment to young Brenda. She had been foisted on him as an assistant by Murdoch and so he carried no direct responsbility for hiring her. While they had slept together, neither of them seemed to take that at all seriously and he did not feel at all proprietorial about her. Well, he thought he did not.

Susan looked a little hurt and, with a pang, Ben worried he might have gone too far. Her eyes appeared to have moistened.

"Fair enough," she sighed at last. "I deserve it. It is hopeless. He is a worm. I am a masochist. I must be."

She bit her lower lip and Ben reached out for her hand.

When Susan began the relationship with Cross it had been a flirtation that had become an adventure. There was no doubt he was an exciting man to be with. For a journalist like Susan, Christopher Cross was where the action was. He delighted in partying almost as much as he excelled at stirring trouble. In a political world populated by dry cynical dullards, he shone as someone with true belief. If nothing else, it was a belief in himself.

Also, she was appalled to admit, an affair with a married man suited her. Such an illicit liaison meant passion without commitment. With a married man she need not compromise her job, her lifestyle or herself by treading the path that might lead to a permanent partner.

Gradually all that had changed. Having an affair meant having only a shrinking share of someone who grew incrementally in importance in her life. Susan was not someone who was used to getting only a small part of anything. She was, she was discovering, an all or nothing girl.

To her disgust she found herself waiting for him. Waiting at home for a call. Waiting at his flat for him to spare an hour for them to be together. Waiting for him to get away from his party, the press gallery crowd or his wife. Too often waiting in vain. The absences fed her anxiety about the situation which, in turn, reinforced her obsession with the man.

Too late she realised affairs were like a marriage. Not to be entered into lightly.

Susan had also begun to wonder whether she liked Christopher Cross. She knew she loved him but lately she had sensed within herself a growing dislike for the way he conducted himself. In the beginning she mistook his cynicism as a sign of how wise he was in the ways of the world. Now, she decided, he was simply bitter. What she had initally thought was a lofty belief in himself was purely an egocentric gift for utterly selfish behaviour.

"What do you do, Benny, when you find your Greek god has feet of clay?" she asked.

"Ah, Greek gods aren't really my sort of thing. You tell your Uncle Benny all about it." He smiled and squeezed her hand more tightly.

Susan looked at him for a long moment. "Not yet, Ben. Not just yet."

He walked with her to the lift. She had a series of stories to write and record for the morning, he had a couple of speeches to redraft. On the campaign trail there was no such thing as an early night.

Across the room, buried deep inside Ben's briefcase, the mobile phone began ringing just after the end of the late news. He ferreted through the stacks of papers and put it to his ear.

"Bradshaw? Cross."

Christopher liked to begin calls brusquely. He had obviously read in some self-improvement book that it established dominance.

"Did you see that?" Cross demanded.

The news had shown an item featuring the Freedom Party being mobbed at a meeting in some rural town.

"When's the last time that old crock of yours ever had that kind of welcome anywhere. Except from bum-kissing fat cats," he crowed. "Those were real people, buddy. My people. My New Zealand. I'm on a roll that's going to take me all the way. You know that now, don't you?"

Ben admitted Cross had a point. The country had fractured into two distinct parts. A largely urban-based grouping of relatively sophisticated, more affluent people and another country, consisting of the elderly, the poor and the provincial, who had not shared in the last decade's economic growth. The first group were smug, secure and selfish. The second were resentful, alienated and brooding.

Other demagogues had risen to power by playing on the fears and jealousies of those who felt others were doing better than they were. Cross was simply applying the lessons of history. He knew there was a rich vein of insecurity in the country, that it felt it needed a strong leader, so he jutted his jaw and attacked soft targets like the rich, Maori, reporters and city liberals.

"It must be so nice for you, Chris, to be that confident of yourself," Ben sighed, leaning back on the pillow. "To be so sure you are always right."

"I am right. You know it," he spat. "I've watched how this country's been run for the last twenty years. I know the people that run it. You don't have to be a genius to do it, they've proved that. I can do it as well as any of them can and it may as well be me as them."

That, in nutshell, was the Cross philosophy, Ben thought. He was a man who lusted after power for its own sake, with no other purpose in mind but to possess control.

"Yeah?" Ben decided to be malevolent. "What if you really screw it up? What if you find it's not as easy as you thought and the Cross miracle doesn't happen? What if you don't have all the answers and those lovely adoring people that wanted to shake your hand today turn on you? Can you handle that?"

Beneath the thick rhinoceros hide of his huge ego, Cross was vulnerable and there lurked the insecurity common to most of us. It was why Christopher habitually used phrases like "you know that" and "you can't deny that". He needed the reassurance that he was right.

It was why he had phoned Ben now. Since the news item was on screen he had probably made several similar calls to people he knew, whose judgement he trusted. Susan's line was most likely tied up as she made her calls to the radio newsroom, so Ben had been the next one in line to get the call.

The challenge worked and the phone went silent for a short while.

"Buddy, you just don't understand, do you? I thought you were a professional. The great spin-doctor," Cross came back. "You have to isolate a readily identifiable enemy. Define him to your supporters. Then, if things do go wrong, you blame the enemy."

Cross was giving Ben a lesson in basic politics.

"If we can't deliver on a promise then we blame the enemy. If we can't boost the pensions because we find we haven't got the cash then we blame the rich for not paying tax or disinvesting in the country or the greedy brown elite who are sucking the lifeblood out of us in Treaty settlements. Get real, Ben! You know as well as I do you can wheedle your way out of anything if you manage the problem well enough. There's always got to be a fall guy to take the blame."

Spin-doctoring could work magic, Ben thought, but there was white magic and black magic.

"Chris, if you follow your logic to its extreme then people end up in cattle cars on a one-way trip to Poland."

"Yeah, well, buddy, there's a few people I can think of would be first on board. Want a drink? I'm in town."

Ben demurred and hung up.

It was just before 1 am and Ben was stacking the sheets of tomorrow's itinerary and the speech notes by the facsimile machine on the desk when there was a sharp rap on the door. He exhaled slowly and leaned his head against the wall for a second before tightening the tie on his hotel bathrobe and reaching for the door nob.

Brenda sprang past and jumped onto his bed, using it as

a trampoline as she spilled her news. "You'll never guess, never in a million years will you guess what he has got," she squealed.

Ben waited and she kept bouncing. He noticed she was not wearing a bra and her rather fetching short black jersey top kept lifting up to expose the magnetic bellybutton.

He dragged his thoughts from the carnal to the political. "Gimme what you got, you little rat."

"Not unless you give me what I want, Benny." She beckoned him with a finger.

It was like dealing with a five-year-old, he thought with exasperation.

Finally, after bribing her with the half bottle of Moet in his mini-bar, he extracted the information from her. George Tyler, one of the Conservatives' Auckland constituency candidates, a city councillor with a strong local following, had a major problem. Three problems, in fact.

The first was that George had got a nineteen-year-old girl pregnant. This was a problem because he was married.

The second was that he had paid for the girl's abortion. This was a worse mistake, for George was a strong public campaigner for family values and had been endorsed by the Christian Crusade Party, who were not standing a candidate against him.

The third problem was that the girl and her mother now felt that George had treated them in a somewhat cavalier fashion and they were now talking to the press in the person of Daniel McGrath. This was the worst of all.

Ben groaned and picked up the phone. Ernie Watts answered sleepily. Politicians and their staff might not sleep but party presidents obviously got their allocated eight hours' rest.

However, a quick outline of the situation regarding the over-active member ensured President Ernie would be sleepless for the remainder of the night.

"You'll have to deal with it, Ernie. The Prime Minister will want his resignation as a candidate by six o'clock in time for *Morning Report* and those petty little inquisitors on the breakfast radio programmes."

He hung up and turned to Brenda, who had collapsed across the bed and was listening with her chin cupped in her hands.

"Good, you're paying attention. A lesson in political tactics. When ambushed by a scandal take immediate and decisive action to avoid a total shafting. Secondly, stage a diversion. And that is where your earlier idea comes in. Tomorrow we pay a visit to the revolting students. By the time the evening news hits our TV screens the saga of the copulating candidate will take second place to the fresher news of the heroic Murdoch's gladiatorial combat with the scarfies. Brenda, I could kiss you."

"Damn fine idea, if you ask me," she cried, pulling his head down to meet her lips.

The clamour in the university quadrangle was deafening. "Murdoch out! Murdoch out! Stop the cuts!" Several hundred bellowing young people surrounded Don Murdoch. He smiled and waved affably, which seemed to incense them more. He was quite alone, apart from a dozen press and television cameramen and two DPS officers who stood two metres away, on the fringe of the ring of encircling students, forefingers pressing the earpieces of their two-way radios closer to their eardrums fruitlessly trying to hear their command signals.

The scene was as Ben intended it to be. Murdoch

standing firm before a mob. Daniel in the lions' den. One man against many, the underdog. It was a picture calculated to gain Murdoch sympathy and admiration for his courage. It was not an entirely original plan. Ben recalled that when the Gennifer Flowers sex scandal broke around Bill Clinton in the presidential primaries for his first term, his staff had deliberately sent him out alone into a howling media mob. He stood his ground and the feeding frenzy of the press revolted the viewing audience. Clinton's support rocketed.

That was Ben's scheme but now, as he confronted the reality, he worried that it could too easily misfire. Murdoch was too exposed: one over-excited student, one individual with more sinister intent, and he could be severely injured.

Oh, great, Ben thought. I've killed my own candidate. In years to come political science classes will study the Bradshaw Balls Up phenomenon, where an eager advisor encourages his political master to publicly commit suicide.

"You tell me what I should do?" The student cries were diminishing in volume and Ben could hear the Prime Minister debating with the students closest to him. "Free tertiary education?" He was nodding in agreement with the suggestion. "Sounds good. Sounds ideal. What degree are you doing? Science. Well, I'd love to fully subsidise your degree. You could contribute a lot to the country, the economy, the well-being of us all. But tell me, Bruce . . . is that your name? Bruce, tell me. Should I also pay for someone doing an arts degree? Yes? But what if that person is, say, doing a fine arts degree to fill in spare time because she or he is married to, say, a wealthy lawyer or a merchant banker? Do you means-test people? Do you find out whether they're studying for a career or self-improvement or as a hobby?"

Murdoch had hit his stride. His young opponent was

losing ground, going redder in the face as his confusion grew. Ben had forgotten how good a debater Murdoch could be. Years of hard in-fighting in the chamber of Parliament had honed his skills in an argument.

The embarrassed young man had fallen silent and several others around him leapt in to quarrel with Murdoch, but regardless of how the argument went he had won. By engaging in discussion the mood had changed from lynch mob to debating society. Those at the back struggled to hear and hissed at those still chanting to be quiet.

The cameras recorded the moment as the hush fell over the demonstration and the impact, when shown later on television, was dramatic.

Murdoch punched the air with a finger. "I'll tell you one thing you are right about. I am concerned at this university's spending. I am concerned at this university's priorities. Its budgeting, frankly, seems to leave a lot to be desired and I want to tell you today I have set up an investigative task force into university spending. I will be asking your association to put forward a representative to be on that task force."

At this there were a few cheers but also some jeers from a hard core of Socialist Party supporters who yelled that it was a smokescreen and a diversion from the real issue of Education cuts.

They were right, thought Ben as he pushed through the throng to get closer to his boss, but it was a damn effective diversion. A hand pulled at his jacket tail and he knocked it away.

"Ow! Benny! That's no way to treat your undercover agents." It was Brenda, who admittedly blended in perfectly amongst the students. He apologised and she laughed.

"I love it when you get rough, darling."

Ben rolled his eyes and turned back to pushing his way through towards Murdoch. Brenda tugged again on his coat.

"You'd better watch out. They were planning to block Uncle Don's exit, to carry him through to the common room and hold him hostage. I listened in to their planning people in the upstairs common room earlier."

"Christ," said Ben. "That'd be a crazy thing for them to do. We've got half the New Zealand police force stashed in vans in the car park below. They'd storm the building in two seconds flat and the students would get their arses kicked from here to kingdom come."

Brenda looked at him with a slightly patronising grin. "That's what they were hoping. Imagine the pictures on the news tonight. You're not the only one who's into manipulating and managing the news, Mr Spin-Doctor. Some of these guys, especially the Socialists, know what they're doing. I go to university here myself, you know?"

Ben began casting around for the head of the DPS, who was watching the confrontation from a balcony high above the quad. Their eyes met and Ben shook his head.

"The inspector wants to send in the boys with the long batons but I think your uncle might just find his own way out of this mess."

Murdoch had, indeed, already figured out the major problem was getting past the student cordon. He had found the student president and wrapped one arm around her shoulder, and was walking with her through the crowd discussing the task force proposal.

Ben frantically signalled the police inspector and pointed at the LTD on the roadside fifty metres away. The cop waved and shouted into a radio microphone on his cuff.

Almost before the student group realised their quarry was about to make his escape, Murdoch was at the limo and a line of uniformed police materialised between him and the crowd. As the cameras focused in close, the Prime Minister warmly shook the student president's hand and Ben barely had time to dive into the back seat before the car and the two police Ford Fairmonts escorting them pulled rapidly away from the kerb.

"What investigative task force into univsersity spending?" Ben yelled as he craned his neck to see the protest spill onto the street behind them.

"Seemed a good idea," said Murdoch.

"Christ, the vice chancellor, the university council and the dearly beloved Minister of Education will be after your guts." Ben was quite stunned at the Prime Minister's audacity at making such a serious policy decision on the hoof.

"Ah, they can go after my guts. Rather them than those young bucks back there who *definitely* wanted my hide. Besides, I'm right. Most councils are grossly inefficient and poor managers. It's about time someone took a close look at how they run their business." Murdoch unbuttoned his double-breasted suit and stretched.

"Did I see that niece of mine in the crowd?' he asked.

"Brenda? Ah, well, yes she was doing a bit of undercover work for us. You know, sounding out the mood of the students. She did a fine job for us actually." Ben guiltily tried to keep the nervousness out of his voice.

"Good. Look after her, Ben, she's very young and quite innocent. Faith is very fond of her and I'd hate for anything to happen to her. Watch out for her with that McGrath character. He wouldn't think twice about seducing a vulnerable girl like Brenda."

A thin bead of sweat had formed on Ben's upper lip. "Absolutely."

"Anyway," Murdoch said, abruptly changing the subject back to his performance with the student mob, "on the whole today, I think that went rather well, don't you?"

11

The Spin

Weeks later, on the Election Night From Hell, elbowing his way through the crowd milling aimlessly in the Tutaekuri hall, Ben recalled that day among the angry student mob. He pressed more urgently through the journalists gathered around the kitchen door. The television cameras swung on to him, a spotlight momentarily blinded him and the cadaverous woman from one of the networks thrust a microphone in his face.

"Ben Bradshaw, the Prime Minister's key strategist is here. Ben, the Liberals and the Freedom Party have already proclaimed they have enough seats to be able to form a Government and they are demanding Mr Murdoch concede. Will he?"

"Gee, what election coverage were they watching?" Ben smiled as he continued to edge through the media scrum. "I thought, between them they were still nearly a dozen seats short of a clear majority? Have the Socialists said they'll join them? I doubt it. I could have sworn the Government won by far the most seats and was by far the majority choice for most New Zealanders?"

Susan Lewis stood squarely in front of him, wearing huge headphones, holding her own microphone towards him. "Ben, when will the Prime Minister let the country in on what he's planning? Is he planning anything at all or is he simply paralysed by the events of the night?"

"You have to appreciate, Susan, this is an extremely sensitive time. The Prime Minister wants to be totally conversant with all the political, economic and constitutional ramifications of tonight's vote before he comes out to brief you, the public and the many, many, supporters of the Conservative Government."

The television woman dropped her shoulder into Susan, throwing her off balance, and pushed in front of Ben again.

"Tell us, Mr Bradshaw. Who is governing the country?" She injected a little theatrical drama into her voice.

Ben edged into a gap in the rolling maul created by the tussle between Susan and the television crew.

"This country has only one Government tonight and for the next two months, till the new Parliament is called." Ben turned his eyes directly into the lens of the television camera behind the reporter. "That is the Conservative Government led by Prime Minister Donald Murdoch and I am confident it will be the Government of New Zealand for the next three years. Excuse me, we have a country to run."

He turned and passed between two of the DPS men who guarded the door. Inside, Murdoch, Faith and Simon Small turned from watching the little television set.

"Who gave you the right to speak for the Government!" Simon's voice was shrill with anger. His eyes narrowed to slits behind the gold-rimmed spectacles. "This Government is finished unless we can get a coalition partner. You have no right to pre-empt . . ."

"Shut up, Simon." Ben's uncustomarily direct rudeness silenced Small for a second. His jaw worked in silent anger.

"Yes. Shut up, Simon," said Faith. It was hard to tell who of the four was most amazed at her outburst in support.

Her husband recovered first. "I've got to agree with them both, Simon. Shut up. Ben did just fine out there. In fact, Benny, you want a list seat next time round?" Murdoch laughed.

"No thanks, Prime Minister. I still have my pride." Ben was burrowing into his battered tan leather briefcase on the table. There was an audible click as a tape slid into his tape-recorder.

Murdoch slapped a hand on his shoulder and said quietly that, however, Small seemed to be right about the need to raise the white flag.

"I'm buggered, Ben. I think I know when to call it a day."

"Before anyone makes any hasty moves, PM, I think it is time for a little game of show and tell. Believe me, this is telling." Ben pushed the play button.

Jane Street's voice echoed through the kitchen. "He must be made to see reason, Simon."

Murdoch listened engrossed to the recorded conversation. Small stood rigid, his blue eyes boring into Ben's. After the segment where Small and Street discussed a leadership coup Ben switched the machine off.

"That is an illegal recording. You have committed a criminal act, Ben. It has no validity." Small was speaking slowly and deliberately.

"So, sue me. We're not in a court of law, Small."

Ben and Simon squared off like gunfighters. It made a slightly ridiculous sight. Two near middle-aged men doing their best Clint Eastwood impressions, legs braced apart, fists clenched, eyeballing each other across a couple of metres of tattered linoleum in the faded yellow kitchen of a decrepit rural village hall.

Murdoch stepped between them. "Enough. You're fired, Simon. Get out." He rapped on the sliding door and Tony, the young detective looked in.

"Tony, this man is fired. His privileges are revoked. Mr Small is now trespassing here. He is to be removed from the hall as quickly and quietly as possible. I don't think you'd want too much media attention, Simon, would you?" Murdoch gestured to the door and Tony took hold of Small's elbow. The grip looked deceptively gentle. Small winced

205

slightly, rose onto the balls of his feet and was propelled out through the mob.

As a distraction Ben stuck his head out and called to the reporters, "The Prime Minister will be making his address to the nation in ten minutes exactly." Small had disappeared by the time they looked back to the front door of the hall. Ben slipped a cassette in Susan's hand.

"Enjoy," he said.

"Benny, what are you up to?" She glanced at the tape and dropped it into her pocket.

"Giving you your long-awaited scoop. Have fun. Broadcast it straight away. We'll be listening." He ducked back inside where Murdoch and Faith stood watching him.

Ben thought he knew the exact moment the ground finally shifted between Susan and him. She told him a secret and a secret shared is a concession of trust. Power irrevocably conceded to another.

She told him how much Chris Cross scared her.

As usual they were in a bar, after midnight. One of the reasons Ben and Susan had become so close without sex intruding was they had shared common interests, including a taste for late-night drinking.

Neither often drank to huge excess. It was as though they needed a certain measure of alcohol to shed the protective barriers they erected around themselves to survive their destructive daily routine.

Journalism could be a brutalising business. There was as much deception, betrayal and plain lying involved in Susan's trade as there was in Ben's openly manipulative game as a political spin-doctor. Less scrupulous people had the kind of character that enabled them to naturally excel in such soulless occupations. Others who possessed a more traditional morality found it debilitating unless they grew a thick outer layer of cynicism that enabled them to play the role.

Susan looked particularly vulnerable tonight, he thought. Dark lids half lowered over her tired eyes, the foundation of her make-up not quite disguising the shadows beneath. She drained her gin and swept back the wall of curls that had veiled her face.

He smiled at her. "Cheer up, this campaign won't last forever. Besides, you are consistently running the best coverage of anyone."

Susan gave her throaty laugh. "Now you've really got me worried. If you say my stuff is good I'm in real trouble. I must be buying your party line, you cunning old bugger."

"Not at all." Ben looked slightly hurt. "In fact, Small wanted you banned from the campaign plane for that vilely insightful piece you did the other day about the *High Noon* showdown on campus. I'm afraid ninety-nine percent of the PM's office now class you firmly in the enemy camp."

"I am as neutral as I can be. I can't help it if your ploys are so easily seen through. And, with my excellent insight, I see I need another of these." She waved her glass and tapped the sleeve of a passing waiter. "Bombay Sapphire and tonic, please."

"Come on, Susie. Don't bite my head off. I mean it when I say you are one of the best political analysts I know. You really have a talent for cutting through the crap. By the way, speaking of crap, since when did you start popping up on *The Holmes Show* as a commentator? I thought you told me television was for wankers and radio was the one medium for a true journalist?"

She sniffed and tried a haughty look as he went on. "Let me see, what was it you told me? 'Radio has the immediacy and the instantaneous impact without the trivialising show-business schtick of the tube.' I thought you managed to survive the corrupting influence of your seven minutes of fame with Paul very well."

"Ha! Very funny. A girl needs a profile, you know. It all helps boost the radio network." She was slightly embarrassed but ignored his teasing, snapping open her handbag to check her face in the mirror of a small black compact. "Besides," she sniffed, "I desparately needed a make-over. Those TV make-up women do wonders."

"Yes and you bought a new frock especially for the occasion, I noticed. Very fetching."

She smoothed the jacket of the lime-green Saba suit and straightened herself. "Why, Benny, you old flatterer. If I didn't know better I'd think you were trying to pick me up."

"What do you think I've been trying to do for the last twelve months?"

"Drink yourself to death."

Standing up with a sigh he reached over and took her hand. "Come on."

"Where? I'm not that little tart Brenda, you know."

He lightly smacked her on the wrist as he led her across the bar and into the hotel's dimly lit restaurant, where Van Morrison's 'Moondance' was playing softly on the empty dance floor. He twirled her around, placed a hand firmly in the small of her back and tightly held her for a quickstep.

"Lord, I'm a sucker for romance," she sighed when he slowed into a more rocking rhythmic pace, laying her head gently on his shoulder.

Laughing, he threw her into a mocking tango, arms stretched forward, leaning her back almost beyond their point of balance. She gave an involuntary shriek which caught the attention of the two businessmen dining in the otherwise deserted silver service room of the restaurant.

The music changed to an old Sinatra number, they slowed into a staid close waltz and her head went back to his shoulder.

"Chris terrifies me, Benny."

If there was one thing Ben Bradshaw had learned in his years in and around the media, it was the value of silence. After a moment she went on.

"He's not a bad man. He's not . . . violent . . . or anything like that."

Ben rocked her to the crooning music.

"But there is an inner violence to Chris. A real dark side to him. You know that. You can feel his anger. It boils away inside like acid, eating him up."

Chris Cross was a man with many grievances. He came from the wrong side of the tracks. Poor white trash was the description he had once used to Susan. Succeeding in high school against all the expectations of the Cross family held by the wider community, Christopher had taken his scholarship and won an accounting degree.

This was, perhaps, his first mistake. Cross always felt like a gatecrasher with the people he now came in regular contact with. Students who were by far his intellectual inferiors gained positions with the big accounting practices and he sensed the door was slammed on him because he lacked the right surname or had not attended the correct College or Grammar.

His background dictated, if he had an interest in politics at all, it should have been with the Liberals or the Socialists. Instead, he gravitated into Tory circles seeking the social legitimacy their company might bring.

The Conservatives were not absolutely elitist. They had always allowed entry to those who strived and succeeded by their own efforts but they could never, by any stretch of the imagination, be described as egalitarian. He was welcomed into the ranks of the party, praised for his energy and finally selected as a candidate for what was presumed to be an unwinnable seat, but complete acceptance was something he felt was denied him.

Later, when he stunned them all by taking the previously safe Liberal constituency seat to enter Parliament, Christopher Cross still felt the invisible walls. He quickly noticed certain members of caucus, with their old boy affiliations, shared investments, insider market tips and the membership of prestigious private clubs. They never invited Cross to participate. When he confronted one backbench colleague and betrayed his lowly origins by crassly demanding a reason, he was told it was because they assumed he did not have the financial resources and no one would want him to over-extend himself. The man was Cross's flatmate at the time.

He felt in his dealings with his many of his party colleagues that they treated him with a slightly mocking, paternalistic condescension. It spurred him to almost super-human efforts in the political arena. He hogged the media limelight, grandstanding mercilessly in the House, accepting any challenge from any rival, no matter how powerful, savaging any target presented by the opposition parties.

This sense of insecurity persisted and was exacerbated by the party's failure to recognise him as leadership material and select him for Murdoch's job.

Several years earlier the party was languishing in

opposition, having lost three elections in a row, still mired at an all-time low in the opinion polls. A couple of backbenchers, men he broadly classed as friends, approached him with the idea of staging a coup against Murdoch. The canny Cross refused to move unless they could present him with a letter signed by more than half of caucus requesting the removal of their existing leader. Not even the two erstwhile conspirators were prepared to commit themselves to the potentially fatal extent of putting pen to paper. If the coup failed they, and anyone else who signed the letter, would be unable to disassociate themselves from Cross.

"Gutless wankers," was the Cross verdict on his colleagues.

Murdoch sniffed the attempt at treachery, checked the polls to find Cross ranking more than twice his own level of popularity in the preferred Prime Minister rating, and exacted a typically petty revenge.

Cross found his puny office staff was cut and his access to the party's research unit drastically curtailed 'for reasons of cost'. Fear of the political cost to Don Murdoch, he realised. He was removed from several key caucus committees, losing his two most important spokesmanships in poor exchange for a couple of mundane tasks in tediously routine areas of policy. The Prime Minister had spent long enough in Parliament to realise how to 'white ant' a potentially dangerous rival. It was a slow death by a thousand little bureaucratic bites.

Angered, Cross fought back. Denied a formal role as a shadow minister, officially restricted to public utterances on minor agricultural matters such as those involving matters like goat husbandry and small seeds and grain, he simply declared himself spokesman on everything. According to the Cross theory, being an MP meant having a democratic obligation to grandstand on every major issue, especially if his own ideas were at variance with the current Murdoch line.

The strategy worked admirably in raising his media profile almost as high as his leader's blood pressure. It also rebounded on him, forever dooming his leadership hopes. Treading on the fragile vanity of his caucus colleagues by upstaging them in their various spokesmanship roles, grabbing the headlines with his own views on their portfolios, soured relations with other Conservative MPs.

Treated as an outsider by the big monied interests who underwrote the party, Cross began targeting them. He developed a speciality in publicly unmasking issues of corporate fraud. His first major success was bringing down a huge public company that had bought a substantial slice of the formerly state-owned gas industry, which had been split into commercial units and sold under tender.

Christopher Cross became a familiar face on the nightly news as he exposed a suspect bidding process and a blatantly fraudulent loan arrangement to underwrite the share float. The scandal rocked the Government of the day but his own opposition party gave him little credit.

Murdoch's bureaucratic pin-prick campaign against him finally became too much. Cross accused him of working hand in hand with big business interests to try and gag him. Murdoch demanded his resignation from the party and a long, involved process of expulsion only guaranteed Cross more headlines.

Finally, he quit before they threw him out, and to his

own surprise found substantial public support for his new Freedom Party. It had the feeling of a crusade, attracting hordes of enthusiastic converts, growing almost without any visible recruitment efforts by Cross.

For any journalist Cross had long been more than just a story. Like some Mario Puzo mafia hitman who would claim an assassination was just business, nothing personal Christopher Cross would spend a day battering a reporter about something they had written, then drink with them all evening.

Early in Cross's career Susan had sensed he had the X factor that could take him to the top and she had cultivated her contacts with him. Their relationship stayed purely professional until the stressful period when he was caught up in the vicious infighting that preceded his resignation from the Conservative Party. They spent hours together, she ostensibly trying to figure out what was going on, he trying to get Susan to angle her coverage in his favour.

After a time he found he was telling her more and she was reporting less. He had generally fought most of his battles alone. "Play your cards close to chest, boy. That was my father's best advice," he told Susan. Yet the sympathetic ear of a woman saw the depressed and worried Cross take sanctuary with her. As Christopher Cross shared his secrets so they grew closer together. Against her better judgement Susan Lewis found herself sharing a bed with him.

In the beginning the affair was marked by passion, fuelled by the fear of discovery, driven by the sheer risk involved. Yet it was impossible to keep such a secret for long in the closed environment of Wellington. Gossip was hard currency in the capital and, before long, it became privately known among the press gallery and political staffers that Cross and Lewis were lovers. The glass house theory prevailed and no one wrote about it or used it in Parliament against him. Too many people had too many sins to cast the first stone.

As the months passed and the initally clandestine affair became a little more public, some of the thrill also went out of it. Cross's career was once again on an upward track with the explosive growth of the Freedom Party and Susan found she rather preferred the depressed Cross to the triumphant one.

While at first his obsession with politics and in particular his own career had fascinated Susan, it dominated all their conversations and after a time began to have all the attraction of listening to a scratched compact disc.

"He is unbelievably selfish, Ben," she said, her face still nestled in his shoulder as they slow-danced. "Vain too. You have no idea of the length of time that man will spend in front of a mirror before he sets out into the world. Every article of clothing must be perfectly ironed, razor sharp creases, the knot in his tie perfect, every blond hair on his head slicked into place."

"That's a reaction to his upbringing," Ben murmured. "Only the rich and the middle class take pride in dressing down. Anyone who has been genuinely poor tries to make the best of his appearance once he's found success."

"Don't make excuses for him. The man is an anal retentitive."

"So am I."

Ben cursed himself for making, on Christopher's behalf, excuses he did not really believe. He lamely tried to explain that she was probably feeling rejected or neglected because of the intense campaign period and that, in a few weeks, the lovers could return to a more stable affair.

"God. Is that it? You think I'm just a whining mistress? Well, you may be right in part. I would like a proper boyfriend. A real lover who can stay the night, come out to dinner parties. Who I can go places with, be seen with, and not have to hide. I'd like to cook him breakfast or, better still, have him cook me breakfast. I would like someone I can plan a future with."

She paused for breath and they stopped in the middle of the parquet dance floor.

"Now, even I am not stupid enough to think Christopher Cross is that man. Even if he left his wife and married me, I would be nothing but an adjunct to him. The well-trained little political wifey. Ugh! No, Ben, I am not complaining about the situation. I am a big girl. I knew what I was getting into with him and, although I may have got carried away for a while, I have found my balance again."

Susan was someone who often had to talk a problem through before she could resolve it. It was as if by verbalising the situation she could talk herself into acting on it. What drove her to this point was less clear.

To Ben's unspoken question she replied, "I'll tell you what my problem is. I don't trust him. I mean it when I say he scares me. He is so bitter and so full of the need to revenge himself on those he sees as his enemies . . . and believe me, Ben, there are many on his enemies list . . . I honestly have huge fears for us, for this entire damn country, if that man gets into power."

They turned and walked slowly back to the booth where they had been drinking, his arm still around her waist holding her close. He spoke softly in her ear. "Maybe you worry too much. You're too close."

"It's because I've got as close as I have that I am worried. You do not realise how cynical and unprincipled he has become."

She picked up her bag from the table and put her hand up to the back of his neck.

"You're a sweet man, Ben Bradshaw. A good man but far too trusting."

What had she found out about Cross, he wondered. Something was gnawing away at her but she was still not prepared to disclose what it was.

"So, what now?" she asked. "You'll be trotting upstairs to that little tart?"

Ben was shocked by the bitter edge to her voice.

"What do you say to a nineteen-year-old, anyway, Ben?"

"Roll over?"

She laughed despite herself. He took her by both shoulders as they waited for the lift and gave her an assurance he thought she might require. "I shall be tucked up in bed, alone, reading the keynote speech to Federated Farmers tomorrow. That should guarantee I'll fall asleep in less than five minutes, alone and unloved."

She planted a warm kiss on his cheek, paused a fraction of a second as if she expected him to make some move, and then stepped back in the lift. The doors closed on her small wave goodbye and Ben shook his head with bewilderment, pushing the Up button again as realised he should have gone in the elevator because his room was on the same floor as hers.

There were three messages waiting for him. One from the Prime Minister's private secretary concerning tomorrow's transport arrangements and two more from Brenda giving a progress report on her tour of the city's clubs and bars with a couple of reporters. He rang the operator, requested no more calls for the evening and unplugged the phone from the wall.

12
The Spin

"Right, Prime Minister," Ben said, briskly striding over to the fridge where the radio sat and flicking it on to the station's election-night broadcast.

"Am I correct in assuming you no longer really give a shit? But you'd quite like to nail as many of the buggers as you can?"

"Succinctly put, Ben. The way I feel right now I don't think any of it really matters much any more." Don threw an arm around his wife's frail shoulders.

"It matters, Don," she said patting his hand. "It matters. You can't let them win like this."

"I'm sick of the backstabbing and all the games involved," he told her. "Especially when I look at what our game-playing did to you. A man gets a shock like that. It makes you think. Reassess your priorities."

Faith craned her head up to his height and met his eyes. "Now you listen to me, Donald Murdoch. Your top priority right now is winning. If you can't win, then the next priority is to make sure those enemies of yours don't either."

Ben walked over and put his arms around their necks and they went into a huddle.

"Well, let's have some fun. You might even end up staying Prime Minister. You trust me?"

Don and Faith exchanged a glance and grinned back. Ben slapped them lightly on the back and picked up the phone.

It rang briefly and a man's voice answered. "Kia ora."

"Congratulations, Luke. The Prime Minister and I would like to extend our heartiest congratulations to you on your victory in Eastern Maori."

Ben glanced across at Murdoch, whose eyebrows were arched while a rueful smile played on his lips. After a few more minutes of gentle fencing, he got to the point.

"Here's the deal, Luke. By tomorrow your party leader will be out of a job. Cross will be disgraced. Gone. If he is not, he should be and you wouldn't want anything to do with a party that kept him as boss."

Faith Murdoch questioningly nudged Don, who shook his head and shrugged.

"I can guarantee that you and several other Freedom MPs won't want anything to do with the party if it retains him as leader." Ben looked at the pair and circled his finger and thumb in a large O. "We're not pulling any dirty tricks, Luke. This is a classic case of Chris shooting himself in the foot, except this time the wound is fatal."

He smiled at the couple who had pulled up chairs and sat like a couple of spectators at a tennis match. Ben nodded quietly to himself.

"I'm giving you this prior information, Luke, because you, above all others, understand that knowledge is power. Right now in this country we have a power vacuum. The knowledge I've given you can help you and those who follow you to fill that vacuum."

There were a few seconds of silence at the other end of the line before Luke grunted and asked exactly what the Government wanted.

"Very little, Luke. Bottom line? What we'd like to know is what you would require to give the Government an assurance you will support it on matters of confidence and supply. You know what I'm driving at. You don't have to go into coalition. All we need is you and half a dozen others to back our minority Government when it comes to such crucial votes in the House."

He paused again and then gestured to Murdoch. "I think the Prime Minister is the man to talk to, Luke. He may well feel the need for a new Minister of Maori Affairs. I'm not sure whether we would require a formal coalition for you to fill that slot."

Murdoch mouthed a "Yes" and Ben gave him the thumbs up. "I think Mr Murdoch might be able to claim that Maori Affairs is a genuinely bipartisan portfolio and it is logical to have an MP from a Maori seat, whatever his party, to occupy the role as Minister. It should be the person's mana that counts, not their party. Talk to the PM."

Murdoch squeezed Ben's shoulder in appreciation and took the phone. "Gidday, Luke? You know I've always had enormous respect for your abilities? I am placing a great deal of trust in you now. Still, you know we are the only Government that will continue to advance the Treaty settlement process. The Liberals would want to but their coalition partner, Mr Cross, will block them. Even with you there pushing for it, Cross will block it."

He listened for a moment or two before nodding in agreement. "Luke, the overall method of settlement, the amounts involved, the nature of the reparations themselves are all open to negotiation. Obviously the party that gave us the support we required in the House would be in a commanding position in those negotiations. Especially if I had you as Minister of Maori Affairs."

The two men talked cryptically for several minutes more. Murdoch grunted as Watene apparently asked what was to prevent him striking a similar deal with the Socialists or the Liberals.

"Simply, Luke, that those parties will be loath to deal with the Freedom Party once news of the upcoming scandal breaks. Now you and half a dozen of the Maori MPs in your party could make a separate break to form your own post election grouping, but that would not give a Socialist-Liberal coalition enough seats to form a Government, would it?"

Watene seemed to agree.

Murdoch asked him what he preferred. To have a voice in Government and achieve something or remain in opposition with little to do but posture. "You'll get some flak when you make the move but Maori are more likely to understand the logic behind your shift than Pakeha."

He went on to explain that by joining in a bipartisan agreement over Maori policy he would be seen to be advancing the interests of the Moari voters who had just elected him.

As he hung up, Murdoch gave Luke Watene a last assurance. "Luke, we don't have to announce this tonight or tomorrow or even next week. You will want to see what occurs with Cross and take the appropriate action within your own caucus. I have given you the tip-off because I know you can be trusted and you will use the warning to marshal your own forces to either deal with the man when he is exposed or walk away from what is in effect a ruined party."

Ben found it hard to resist a small smile at that. Murdoch still did not know what hidden card his spin-doctor held yet he made the statement with utter confidence.

"All I need is your undertaking that, when what we've told you comes to pass, and it will, you will back us when Parliament resumes in the first week of December."

He grunted with satisfaction at Watene's reply.

"Done deal, Luke. We thank you and the country will too." Murdoch hung up.

"Now, Ben, I think I follow most of what is going on here. We've got Watene and half a dozen of his Maori MPs onside, so long as Christopher Cross commits political suicide. Now that is a huge punt. I presume he will, Ben? You're not bluffing are you?

Admittedly he was not a great poker player. It was one of his many minor vices. Ben had been nearly two hundred dollars down in a hot game at his old Wadestown villa ten days earlier when the phone rang shortly after 11 pm.

It was Susan. He could tell by her strained tone that something was seriously wrong but Susan merely said she needed to hear a friendly voice and apologised for interupting his male bonding session.

The habit of the fornightly card school had been a running gag between them, Susan claiming it was an elaborate cover story for men too macho to admit they were in therapy and holding an encounter group.

Ben was always wrong-footed by her teasing. One of the card school regulars was a former brother-in-law who happened to be a psychiatrist and over the course of the evening, in between the jokes and the bids, the men did talk more openly about their lives than they would generally have revealed in any other social setting.

"Are you at home?" he asked. "I'll come round."

He did not listen to her when she claimed it was not necessary. The card sharks hooted with derison when he cashed in his chips with a hasty apology and grabbed his favourite old denim jacket from the back of the bentwood chair.

"Lock up after yourselves. Don't drink all my beer, and do the dishes." He grabbed the car key off an old rimu desk in the living room.

Good-natured catcalls and ribald speculation on the possible carnal motives behind his departure followed him down the stairs to his garage.

The old Porsche purred sweetly along the waterfront past the wharves and when he hit the long straight heading towards the railway station he briefly floored the accelerator, enjoying the high whine of the engine as the car shot past slower traffic.

The blast of speed calmed him. Whatever had rattled Susan this evening he bet her lamentable lover was to blame. Worry about Susan and her dead-end affair had consumed him for several days now and earlier that morning he had rung Christopher Cross on a pretext.

The Freedom Party leader took the call on his speaker phone, a rude habit that Ben distrusted intensely. It meant there was almost certainly someone else other than Cross listening at that end and it was likely Chris was big-noting to some staffer about the way he dealt with lackeys of the Prime Minister.

"What do you want, Bradshaw?" Cross snapped, his voice tinny and echoing from the effect of the speaker.

"Just calling for a chat, Chris, now that the campaign is picking up some steam. I see the Liberals think you're a certain coalition partner for them."

"That bloody Foot is dreaming. Who does he think he's fooling?" Cross roared. "If he's lucky I might invite him to join my Government. Who does he think he is? Have you seen how they're rating in the polls? What makes the Liberals think they'll be the senior coalition partner?" The questions were fired down the line in a staccato fashion.

Ben laughed. The Liberals would never countenance playing second fiddle to Cross. If he held the largest number of seats Foot and the Liberals would rather remain in opposition and let Murdoch limp on as a minority Government. Cross did not want to hear.

"You wait, Bradshaw. They'll be on their knees on election night, begging for my help. You guys will be too. Well, you might just find that I'm in the driver's seat and you'll just have to wait to find out my terms."

"Well, Chris," Ben put in, "you could always say a plague on both your houses and jump into bed with Knox and the Socialists."

"That liar. He'll get his just deserts. You can't trust the Socialists. They're all little bloody Trotskys waiting to stab you in the back."

"Actually, it was Trotsky who got stabbed with an icepick, Chris."

"Don't lecture me, Bradshaw. We'll see who's consigned to the dustbin of history in two weeks time."

They duelled for a few minutes longer until Cross suddenly became increasingly suspicious.

"Are you taping this? I bet you are. I know your people are following me around. The police or the SIS. Some Government stooge organisation is tracking me constantly, bugging my phones, intercepting my mail. You won't find anything, Bradshaw. Tell your boss that."

"I think you're being overly sensitive, Chris . . ." Ben began.

"You think I'm stupid or something?" he interrupted with a yell. "I know the monied interests and powerful forces that I have offended. My presence in this election threatens their very existence and they'll do anything to stop me."

Ben held the receiver further away from his ear as Cross built up a head of steam on the subject.

"But I won't be stopped, Bradshaw. Not by them, not by you and certainly not by that blockhead of a boss of yours. I stand for New Zealanders, real New Zealanders, and we're on the march. We're going to take this country back, we're going to reclaim our freedom . . ."

He was in full campaign speech flow and Ben maliciously decided to cut off the torrent. "So how's Susan?" he asked.

Cross snatched the receiver of the phone and the speaker was switched off. "Listen to me, Bradshaw," he spat. "You try that crap on me in this campaign and you'll be sorry. I know plenty of dirt on a lot of people in this place and I won't hestitate to drop it."

Ben was taken aback. "Chris. We're old friends. No one's threatening you on this. It was simply a question. You're being paranoid . . ." He never got the chance to finish as Cross slammed the phone down.

Later that night, turning the black snout of the Porsche up the driveway to Susan's Oriental Bay apartment, he wondered if he had somehow turned Cross's paranoid rage onto Susan with that question. He also could not help but wonder if he had done so deliberately.

She answered the door, gave a weak smile and beckoned him in.

"Lord. I must be important to you if you walked out on your encounter group, sorry, poker game. I hope you and your other little card-playing buddies won't regress or go into denial, whatever the psychological jargon is."

He faked slashing his wrists and sprawled on the couch taking in the panoramic inner-harbour view.

"How on earth do you afford the rent on something like this, Susan?"

"Well, I'm surely not a kept woman," she laughed. "That's one thing you can't accuse me of. If you must know, I have rich flatmates. Or, more precisely, an Aussie diplomat who has an extremely good accommodation allowance. You know they class Wellington as virtually as a hardship post and pay them a fortune just to live here and work in the High Commission?"

"Typical Australians. They'd do that just to prove a point about how superior they are," Ben grunted. "So, Susie, what's the matter? Tell your old Uncle Benny."

She asked if he had talked to Christopher that day and shifted guiltily when he admitted he had.

"He said you tried to blackmail him, Ben, over me." She turned a full inquisitorial stare on him.

"Crap."

She stayed silent.

"Crap!" said Ben more emphatically. "I asked him how you were. His paranoid brain went into conspiratorial overdrive and he went ape."

She walked slowly away, slid open the ranchslider onto the deck and asked him outside. They leaned on the rail, looking down at the yachts in the brightly lit marina below.

"I believe you," she said at last. "You called him paranoid before. You know, I truly believe he is. If he is not paranoid, he is at least seriously disturbed."

Ben mentioned a newspaper article he had seen where a professor of psychology at a British university had produced a study showing psychopaths and politicians share many similar traits. Paranoia, a total lack of scruples, an utter inability to express shame or remorse, an absolute belief in their own superiority and the infallible correctness of their position. Neither psychopaths nor politicians could ever admit when they were wrong. Susan decided the description was perfect for Cross.

"Why are we standing out here freezing, Susan?" Ben

asked, hunching his shoulders, tucking his hands in the denim pockets of his jacket.

"Habit. Because I'm almost as paranoid as he is now." She shook her hair off her face and looked at him, explaining she and Cross discussed nothing inside the flat any more because of his fear of bugs.

Ben was certain there was no Government-inspired surveillance on Cross. He had been toying with the idea of bringing in some freelance spooks to monitor cellular phone traffic on election night but, so far, there were no black operations underway.

The cellphone listening post could be justified once polling ceased on the grounds it did not interfere with the voting process but gave the Government early warning of any constitutional or financial threats to the country in the unstable hours following an election. Anyway, that was how he rationalised it to himself. Actively mounting covert operations against political opponents during the running of an election campaign was too reminiscent of the Nixon years for Ben to seriously consider. Besides, someone might find out and, like Nixon, Murdoch would be doomed.

He supposed it was possible that Cross had made some serious enemies from the fund scandal and his attacks on big business. These people were rich enough and powerful enough to mount their own dirty tricks campaign against him.

Susan gave a bitter laugh. "There is no danger of that. Chris might like to posture about being the lone crusader and paint himself as having these big, heavy enemies, but it is all bullshit. Perhaps part of him wants to believe it or really does think it's true, but the rational side of his brain must tell what the reality is."

Puzzled, Ben asked her why, but she ignored him and explained what had happened when Cross had called round earlier in the evening.

He had ranted about Ben's supposed efforts to blackmail him and had insisted they were close to being publicly unmasked. He warned her of the repercussions should she be crazy enough to go public with the story.

"Like I'm going to ring *Woman's Day* and pour out my heart to them?" She was quivering with suppressed anger. "What does that guy think I am? And then he threatens me."

When cornered Christopher Cross was an extremely dangerous man. He claimed to have several ex-SAS men for his own special security. Should she ever betray him, he warned, she would have to answer to these men.

Susan had laughed at this.

"That is it, I thought. We're through. I can put up with his selfishness, his vanity, his all-consuming ambition, his lack of real human feeling and his utterly amoral behaviour, but when he starts questioning my loyalty and physically threatening me that is it. He's out of here!" She sounded a lot stronger than Ben suspected she really was at that moment.

They walked back inside the apartment and across the dark-stained timber floor to the door.

"Thank you, Ben. I feel better having got all that off my chest."

He kissed her lightly on the forehead and she caught her breath. "Wait here." She disappeared into her bedroom and returned carrying a large yellow envelope. "Something left at my place by the fairies. Actually, a very forgetful paranoid fairy who is about to get what he deserves. Add this to your X-Files, Benny. This is the X-File to end all X-Files."

The Spin

She pushed him out the door before he could ask any more questions and he sat in the Porsche, several floors below the apartment, reading the file before driving home to the remains of his poker evening.

13

The Spin

"You're not bluffing are you?"

"Absolutely not, Prime Minister." Ben reached into the briefcase again and pulled out a tattered red cardboard folder. "The last and greatest X-file." He passed it across to the Prime Minister, who opened the yellow envelope inside the folder and spread a sheaf of photocopies across the kitchen table.

"These are Xerox copies of several bank accounts. The first are four Freedom Party accounts. In each of the Freedom Party account balance sheets you'll see for the last six months a series of large regular deposits from one individual account. The Ward Trust. That is to say, Joey Ward."

Ward was a legend in political circles. Retired and in the dotage of his eighties now, twenty years before he had been a powerhouse of New Zealand business, amassing a huge fortune. He had dabbled in politics over the years, backing various Governments when their policies coincided with his own eccentric interests. Little had been heard of him since he had retired several years ago, although the names of him and his fearsome socialite wife surfaced from time to time in connection with various philanthropic causes.

It appeared, from the bank records, the philanthropist had decided to become a huge benefactor to Christopher Cross and the Freedom Party.

Murdoch shook his head. "This isn't enough, Ben. So mad old Joey Ward decides to hurl his fortune into the Freedom Party. So what? He's old money, he's not one of the big-money boys Cross has been attacking. This will all come out in a few months when the parties hand over lists of their donors to the Electoral Commission. No one's going to get too wound up about Joey Ward bankrolling the Freedom Party."

Ben reached into the pile of papers and flourished another fat wad of balance sheets.

"There is one other bank account and these records won't go to the Electoral Commission. These are copies of the monthly statements for the Joseph Ward Trust Account. You'll recall this is the one paying money to the Freedom Party accounts. It looks like Cross may not have entirely trusted old Joey and wanted to see the records of his accounts to check nothing was going astray."

Murdoch looked confused and Ben led him through the money maze.

"You see, old Joey was just the front man. Even he couldn't afford the kind of bucks that have been pumped into Cross. Joey was the filter, the laundry for other donors."

To avoid exposing their sources of corporate money, Freedom fundraisers were funnelling the cash through Ward's account to keep their donors at arm's length. They had committed a mistake: they had put the donors onto an easy payment plan to the Ward Trust. Instead of one big cheque, many of their biggest donors were on a monthly automatic payment system.

"Now, that's not a bad idea," conceded Ben. "The party can budget knowing it has a revenue stream and the donors know they can turn off the tap, cut off the funds, if the party goes off on the wrong policy track."

Murdoch pursed his lips. "Not a bad idea at all. We should try that."

"One downside, Prime Minister. With automatic payments the name of the donor making the deposit shows up on the Ward Trust's monthly statement. Check out the names putting cash into the Trust's account."

Murdoch ran his finger down the left-hand side of the

ledger as Ben continued his lesson. "Some of them are shelf companies but I got my gophers to do a few company searches and establish who was behind them. It reads like the Business Who's Who of the country's top fifty companies. I bet if we traced back the first deposits they would roughly coincide with Christopher's sudden silence on foreign investment. When did you last hear him pounding the podium on issues like labour reform, tariffs or increased personal and company tax?"

Ben ran his finger to the date at the top of the first Freedom Party balance sheet. "I bet you'll find those policy attacks stopped around the tenth of April, about the same time the first big payment came through the funnel from the Ward Trust."

Murdoch whooped with delight and agreed the evidence of the bank statements was enough to ruin Cross. The Freedom Party crusader had campaigned on a platform of bluster about the big-business conspiracy that secretly pulled the Government's strings. When the rank and file of his party saw the depth of his deception, that he had been accepting donations from the very men he was supposedly promising to bring to heel, whose assets he was promising to nationalise or reclaim for the state, Chris Cross would be lynched.

Murdoch sat back and stared at his advisor.

"Jesus, Benny. God bless you and your X-Files."

"Now it's time for you to get out there and kick some arse." Ben gestured at the door. "Pardon the language, Faith." He cocked an ear. "But first, check out this sweet music."

From the old valve radio perched on the bench they heard a replay of the now familiar Street-Small tape.

Murdoch looked out of the corner of his eye at Ben.

"Simon was right on one thing. That tape's illegal, you know. Your Miss Lewis could get in serious trouble playing it."

"The radio network faces, at worst, a wee fine under the Post Office Act or something like that. I don't think Small or Street will be suing. They couldn't afford even more scandal, Don."

Murdoch did not show any reaction to the unaccustomed familiarity. He reached out for the phone and dialled the personal private secretary in the communications room. There was a distinct clank from a cleaner's bucket as Ronald leapt to grab the receiver.

"Get me the Governor of the Reserve Bank, please." There was a short delay while the call was put through but there then followed a rapid fire conversation that left Ben thinking he had not seen Murdoch so full of energy since their first victory night celebration in the same hall years ago.

The Governor was obviously feeling the increasing strain of Holt's treacherous assault on the dollar. The rest of the trading banks were staging a fighting retreat, trying to protect their own dollar holdings as best they could.

"I appreciate your independence, Governor, but I am telling you of my intentions because they are vital to your strategy in defending the Kiwi dollar. I will not concede. If necessary I will continue to govern as a minority Government. However, I believe I will soon be able to weld together a majority coalition. I am confident of the support of a sizable grouping from one of the opposition parties." He glanced at Ben and winked. "Within the next twenty-four hours the identity of that voting bloc should become apparent to someone of your political intuition." He waved and crossed his fingers at Faith, who smiled and crossed her own.

"The point is this, Governor. This run on the dollar has

done farmers like me a huge favour and our exporters will have a couple of months to reap the benefit before fully renewed economic confidence bounces the value of the dollar back up again. Politically we are in for a slightly unstable time but it is nowhere near as a bleak as it might look tonight. My advice to you is take no precipitate action for another forty-eight hours." He grinned and hung up.

"Next, the Governor-General."

In the caretaker's office on the other side of the hall Ronald frantically fumbled through his carefully prepared list of numbers and dialled the Vice-Regal number.

"Mate!" Murdoch boomed into the phone. "Don't you go letting anyone try and form a Government without talking to me first."

He laughed and the pair chatted amiably.

A few minutes later he put the receiver down, reached out his hand and pulled Faith gently to her feet. "Let's go, dear. We have a victory to celebrate."

The cacophony of noise in the hall doubled and then trebled as the Murdochs pushed their way through the media that crowded their approach to the stage and the roar of the party supporters drowned out screamed questions from the reporters. Murdoch laughed and shook his head, cupping one hand to his ear, his other arms remaining tightly around Faith's thin waist as she was buffeted by the wave of journalists.

Cheering wildly, the rest of the crowd climbed on tables, chairs and any other vantage point to get a glimpse of the couple who were all but hidden by the media. Ben glanced up at the huge video screen on the wall and saw a close up shot of a manic Brenda in a sea of bodies, sitting on someone's shoulders like she was at a rock concert, clenched fists punching the air, laughing and screaming at the top of her ample lungs. He cast around and saw her across the room, swaying sideways towards the stage.

Don and Faith emerged onto the raised platform, dwarfed by their own giant images on the video screen beside them. Hands raised and linked in triumph the pair moved toward the podium microphone.

Gradually the crowd grew quiet but Murdoch set them roaring again when he bellowed into the microphone.

"Anyone who thought they were going to hear a concession speech is wrong. Dead wrong!"

It took a full minute for the roar to die down and the crowd gained more hope as Murdoch went on.

"Don Murdoch and the Conservative Party Government is here to stay for another three years!"

When that burst of cheering ceased Murdoch's eyes found the key camera that was carrying his image into the nation's homes. "You elected this Government. We have by far the largest number of seats in Parliament. I am confident of the mature assistance of a sufficient number of opposition MPs to allow us to govern this country for another three years. You have my promise on that."

The ovation was deafening but Murdoch stilled them with an outstretched hand.

"It won't be the kind of Government we have been. The electorate sent us a clear message of rebuke. Justifiably so. We have been unduly harsh, in some quarters. Unduly rigorous, unnecessarily dogmatic on matters of doctrine. In short, we lost our common sense. I want to assure New Zealand that we have regained our common sense. Our humanity may, at times . . . *was* at times, lost for petty political reasons. No more."

The crowd had lapsed into silence, sensing some extraordinary shift was occurring. Dramatically lit by the television lights, possibly for the first time in his career Murdoch seemed to carry a substantial presence.

In tune with the change of mood, his voice became softer as he explained Jane Street had tendered her resignation from his Cabinet and from the Parliament. Her position as a party list MP would be automatically filled by the next candidate on the list. There was a pause then the cheering began again.

A hint of a smile played on the Prime Minister's lips and Ben laughed inwardly. This announcement would be the first Street knew of her resignation. Murdoch had finally figured out how to fire someone. State as fact that she was quitting and she would find it hard to deny or fight back since the embarrassing revelation of her stillborn coup. The Street-Small tape had done the rounds of the chooks in the last half hour and had been played on television just before Murdoch took the stage.

He showed his impressive powers of retention when he launched into a speech Ben had crafted for him months before for another occasion. It was all about putting the heart back into the country and back into Government, giving birth to the generosity of spirit that once had been the hallmark of the nation. Simon Small had vetoed the speech as "negative to Government policy" but, while it was certainly a little saccharine, at the time both Ben and Murdoch had been fond of its message.

When the Prime Minister stepped down from the stage he was mobbed by the crowd and the media, who wanted still more, but Murdoch pressed his way through to where Ben stood grinning by the kitchen door. The two men stared at each other for a long second before Murdoch unexpectedly reached out and gave Ben a Boris Yeltsin-style bear hug.

"What do you reckon, Ben?"

"Not bad, Don, but you've still got a hell of a long way to go. Luke might back out. Knox and Foot might kiss and make up. Cross might resurrect himself – you can never write him off."

"Ah, bugger them. If we have to we'll give it a go by ourselves as a minority Government and see if they have the balls to take us out. Whatever happens, we'll give it a go. You and me." Murdoch still had one arm around him.

There was a short hestitation from Ben. "Actually, Don, once we've sorted out who's who and what's happening, after Christmas, I thought I might try something else for a while. You know, make a documentary or two, do a bit of public relations maybe, perhaps write a book." He almost shuffled his feet in embarrassment but managed to meet Murdoch eye to eye.

"Fair enough, Benny. You've done us proud. I couldn't ask for more I suppose. If we're still around we'll look after you. What do you know about Pest Control?"

They laughed and Don Murdoch turned around towards the wall of reporters being held back by the detectives. "I'd better go and feed the chooks I suppose. Still," he asked as he moved away, "I think that all went rather well, don't you?" He chuckled and raised his arms in triumph and parted the wall of police to greet the waiting media.

Hours later when the post-mortems were over, the lights finally dimmed and the technicians were coiling their cables, Ben picked his way through the litter of another election night.

Smoking a cigarette, Susan Lewis leaned against the

weatherboards underneath the lamplight of the front
entrance.

"Gutt eveningk big boy, vant a voman?" she purred.

"Marlene! Darling! You look divine tonight." Ben could
do a reasonable matinee idol impression when required.

"Stop horsing around, fool, and take me to bed."

The speed of their transit across the wet tarseal road to
the old Tutaekuri pub opposite would have looked a little
undignified if anyone had seen.

Upstairs, in the dark they both squeezed in to the small
single bed, a pink candlewick bedspread pulled up under
their chins against the dampness of the tiny room, listening
to a raucous party in the lounge bar below.

"Thanks for the tape," she whispered.

"Fair exchange, my sweet." He kissed her neck. "Why did
you finally give me the bank records?"

Susan pulled her head away and looked at him
incredulously.

"For someone who has been married as often as you
have, you don't really understand women at all, do you? Or
maybe that's why you've been through as many wives as you
have."

He blinked uncomprehendingly and she lowered her
forehead onto his shoulder. "I had to break free. That seemed
the cleanest, easiest way. Besides, the swine deserved it."

They giggled quietly until Susan suddenly remembered
something. "What did you do with the file?"

"I poked a copy under Danny McGrath's door across the
corridor here. If and when he ever gets back from the post
match party he will find he has a scoop."

McGrath's scream of delight woke them both shortly
after 2 am. They thought they could hear him talking

feverishly to a woman who sounded suspiciously like the Prime Minister's niece.

"I suppose that was his reaction to the file and not his mounting pleasure with young Brenda?" Ben asked.

"It's the file, Ben. Brenda's too young to know how to make a boy that happy," the older woman laughed, and proceeded to show him what she meant.